SCHOOLED!

A NOVEL BY

MATTHEW ROCKWOOD

Based on one lawyer's true-life successes, failures,
frustrations, and heartbreaks while teaching
in the New York City public school system.

Matthew Rockwood

Schooled!

Print ISBN: 978-1-54391-497-9

eBook ISBN: 978-1-54391-498-6

PROLOGUE

The experience of teaching in a failing public high school as part of the New York City Teaching Fellows program is something that I have wanted to write about for some time—and if you are reading this, I guess I eventually got around to it.

Most of the events this novel is based upon took place between 2002 and 2005, yet I delayed writing this book for several years, partly because I felt I needed some distance from the experience to make better sense of everything that happened. After my three years participating in the Teaching Fellows program and teaching English at an inner-city public high school, I left the New York City public school system, burned out and discouraged, but with a much greater appreciation for the challenges of the profession and for the complexities of the problems facing many of our public schools.

I continued my teaching career at the community college level where I gained, in some ways, an even more frightening perspective of the damage that can be done by our dysfunctional public school system. I've seen firsthand the harm caused by a system that all too often graduates students who can't read with meaningful comprehension, write coherently, perform basic research, pass a college-level math course, or think critically.

And those are the graduates.

The majority of the students who attended the public high school where I did most of my teaching didn't graduate—and I can only imagine where they are today.

Another issue I faced was that I wasn't sure what form of book I wanted to write. Although I originally considered a nonfiction approach, I soon realized that through a fictional work I could write with the freedom that would allow me to paint a better picture of what it was like to teach at a failing New York City public high school and to better impart to the reader some of the larger issues I believe face public education in this country.

So it is important for the reader to note that, although this book is inspired by true events, it is a work of fiction. I have taken poetic license to combine actual events together and to change certain particulars. And, in some instances, I have included events that are plausible but fictional.

I have also chosen not to include the actual names of the schools where I taught, although their general descriptions are similar to their real-life counterparts (there is no Earl Warren High School or Benjamin Harrison High School in New York City at the time of this writing).

The reader should also understand that all the characters in this novel are fictional and that any resemblance to actual persons living or dead is purely coincidental. While the students depicted look and act similarly to many of the children I had the privilege of teaching, none are based on real people. Likewise, none of the teachers, administrators, or teaching fellows depicted are based on the real-life teachers, administrators, and teaching fellows I had the pleasure of working with. And while my protagonist James Hartman and I are both attorneys who chose to teach at a struggling New York City public high school, our characters are different in many ways (both personally and in our professional lives), and he is not meant to be me.

I also don't want to imply that because of my experience I somehow have all the answers (I wish I could offer definitive solutions to the problems facing our nation's public schools, but I can't). I can say with certainty that the issues are complex and the solutions to these problems must be equally thoughtful and, in some cases, radical.

I don't believe real change will happen without a fundamental (and in many ways controversial) restructuring of the system—and even then societal issues which go well beyond the classroom (such as the influence of street gangs, teen pregnancy, lack of parental involvement, and many other issues associated with the great socioeconomic inequality we have in this country) will continue to cause problems in public schools serving the underprivileged.

I can also say with confidence, based upon my experience both as a teacher and as a parent of children in public school, that the simple solutions often touted by our political leaders on both sides of the aisle will only serve to perpetuate—and in many cases weaken—a crumbling system.

Although the reader will come away with the conclusion that our public school system (and to a larger degree, our society) is very broken, it is also important to understand that many parts of the public school system are worthy of great praise. Many of the teachers and administrators I worked with cared deeply for their students and routinely went well beyond what the system required for the benefit of their kids. Many were also very good at what they did and were professional, even in the midst of what was often, literally, chaos.

And despite all the problems with the system, there are some good public schools. My own children have attended several of them.

Finally I hope this book underscores that our public school system, particularly where it serves our children who are most at need, must be fundamentally changed—not just for the sake of the many good kids it leaves behind—but for our society—which loses the potential of every student the system fails—potential which could benefit us all.

CHAPTER 1

BUBBLES

"Just sit back and collect your paycheck!"

"We ain't gonna do your work anyway!"

"You ain't doin' no good here!"

The new teacher tried to put on a brave face. "I don't believe that. I believe that education is the cornerstone of..."

"Books is wack!"

"School is wack, yo!"

"You just a babysitter till we sixteen—then we outta here!"

The kids laughed as crumpled balls of paper sailed across the classroom.

The next scene had the teacher retreating to the faculty bathroom in tears.

"Overblown Hollywood dramatics," James Hartman muttered to himself, alone on a Friday evening in mid-December of 1997 as he focused his attention away from the small television playing the late movie and back to the many textbooks and notes from his first-year law courses that surrounded him. He tried to find a more study-inducing position on the never comfortable 80's-era dormitory-style couch which was, like the other school-provided furnishings that dotted the room, desperately out of place in the wood-paneled common area of his cramped, two-bedroom "suite" in the stately but badly dilapidated residence hall for law students at the university.

You have to stop distracting yourself, James admonished as he picked up his textbook on contracts and attempted to focus on the case in front of him—the famous one about the hairy hand and expectation damages that his contracts professor emphasized during the first week of class. He'd already read the case six or seven times, but no matter how hard James studied, it never seemed like it would be enough to prepare him for his first law school exams, which were just days away now.

Indeed, James's dutiful and practically nonstop preparation from day one of the semester had only made him feel less confident. There was so much material and seemingly endless ways to interpret case law that for the first time in his life, James was unsure of how he would do academically—or if he would even pass! But more frighteningly, he was beginning to question—ever more increasingly as exam week approached—if he even belonged in the legal profession at all.

It was no use—his mind was shot. James closed the textbook and focused back on the movie, which had gotten to the part where the students trash the poor teacher's car. He'd seen the film before. It would be a tough road, but the new teacher would eventually bridge the gap between their world and the world of their inner-city students—and would, in the end, make a difference in their lives. Even if the movie was a bit exaggerated and had a far too Hollywood ending for James's taste, James found that it was making him think about his life again.

Was law school the right choice? Maybe he should have tried something like the teacher in the movie—tried going outside his comfort zone to make a difference in the world instead of chasing after the pot of gold at the end of the law school rainbow.

Perhaps his roommate Chad "the big shark" Hunter had been right when he made the remark during one of their more impassioned political debates at the beginning of the semester—about a story on the evening news concerning Wall Street greed and economic inequality—that James was far too much of an idealist to be a successful lawyer.

"I feel sorry for you, bro. Life isn't fair or just, and nobody can make it that way. Do you want to make money, or do you want to be some schmuck going broke trying to save the world doing some public defender nonprofit bullshit?"

Chad usually did most of the listening during their frequent and usually playful debates while James did most of the actual debating— James taking them much more seriously than his laid-back classmate. But Chad was more reflective than usual that evening back in September, and in an almost somber tone added, "If you want to be a successful attorney, James, you're going to have to grow up and accept the world for what it is. Otherwise, just drop out now and save yourself a lot of grief."

Chad's comment had hung in the air as the two had just stared at each other, Chad nearly as surprised by his uncharacteristically blunt assertion as James had been. But Chad had quickly laughed it off, opened a beer, and returned to his usual, less serious self. "Or just stay and don't give so much of a fuck. And then we can make tons of money—right, bro?"

James had laughed along with Chad at the time but had privately wondered whether Chad—a guy with all the advantages who had been groomed his whole life to be a lawyer and follow in his father's footsteps defending white-collar criminals of the Wall Street variety—actually knew what he was talking about.

Perhaps he did care too much for his own good. Perhaps an interest in the subject and fondness and skill for debating all things political weren't enough to succeed in law. What if he wasn't the right type of person to make it in the profession?

James got up and opened the window. The sudden rush of cold air made him feel better—more alive again. He could hear the laughter and screams of delight of the undergraduates in the quad beneath him as they frolicked in the first snow of fall, which James had hardly noticed during his daylong marathon study session. He slowly ran his finger along the cold, piled-up whiteness along the outside windowsill, burrowing out a long path in the new snow that he imagined to be his life. And he wondered if it would be worth it to spend much of that lifetime in an office at a law firm where he would miss the beauty of too many snowy days.

He should have tried working at a law firm first, before doing what seemed "practical" for a liberal arts major like himself—going straight to law school. He should have seen what life was like inside that bubble—the bubble of the legal profession—and whether it was really the bubble where he wanted to spend the rest of his days.

Bubbles, James thought as he closed the window and returned to the couch to finish the movie. That was the teacher's problem too. The students and their teacher came from completely different worlds and simply couldn't relate to one another at first.

James wondered if he would have a similar problem working at a law firm filled with people like his roommate Chad—people who accepted the world for what it was and were too "grown up" to expect they could ever change it for the better. Would he be able to adjust to life in such a bubble? Or should he have found another bubble inhabited with people more like himself?

Bubbles: different careers, different values, different life experiences... James amused himself with the notion that perhaps life itself boiled down to bubbles.

Biology was about bubbles—bubbles called cells—trillions of which interacted, arranging themselves into a larger bubble perceived as a living organism.

Sociology was the study of groups of those larger bubbles called human beings, interacting and forming larger bubbles—institutions, neighborhoods, cities, and countries. James's law school was an example of such a bubble—containing some of the most privileged, self-centered, bubbleheads to be found anywhere.

Economics studied the life and death of bubbles: expanding bubbles made people rich, and exploding bubbles wiped them out.

Psychology analyzed the electrochemical conversations of the hundred billion interconnected bubbles networked together inside the bubble in which we all live—the human skull.

And James had even read that some cosmologists believed the basic construction of everything that was—and everything that ever would be—was really just a vast, ever-forming multiverse of bubbles.

Perhaps this explained young children's fascination with bubbles. Children instinctively understood at some level what life was all about—before growing up, losing their innocence, and focusing on the pursuit of money and status as providing meaning in their lives instead of the fun, floaty things that really mattered.

James thought about his own childhood and the bubble he grew up in—a rather exclusive and isolated one—as, perhaps, all bubbles are. His bubble was the Upper West Side of Manhattan in the 1970s and 1980s—home to families that mostly considered themselves upper middle class—but would probably have been considered well-to-do in most other parts of the country.

James, like many in his world, had gone to expensive private schools and lived a somewhat sheltered existence—much like the teacher in the movie James was still half watching. He had well-meaning but over-involved parents who, like many parents in this particular bubble, provided their children with all the best toys from FAO Schwartz and designer clothing and shelves full of books and summers in rented beach houses on Fire Island in James's case.

And his parents were good educational role models who had gone far in school and valued academia. His mother was an editor and a writer—working freelance during the latter half of her career so she could devote more time to motherhood now that James had finally arrived after so many years of trying. His father was ten years older—a doctor—one of a dying breed of general practitioners that still maintained a small practice on the Upper West Side.

Both had always taken for granted that their only child would go to college.

Indeed, the assumption in James's world was that James and most of his friends and acquaintances would go—not just to college—but would go to the *best* colleges and the *best* graduate schools according to *US News and World Report.*

And the majority would pursue well-paying careers in a narrow set of white-collar professions—sometimes at the expense of other important but unrelated interests that got in the way.

It was the one serious disagreement James ever had with his usually overly supportive parents—his intention to continue one of those unrelated interests—his beloved swimming—in college.

His father was particularly adamant. "Do you realize the time commitment at the college level? You're not going to the Olympics, so why put your entire career path at risk for the sake of a sport?"

James had been captain of his high school swim team—a big fish in the small pond of New York City prep schools where academics usually took precedence over sports—diversions which were considered by most in that world to be good extracurricular activities to list on one's college applications but only to be seriously pursued in exceptional cases.

But James had refused to give up swimming in college—barely making the team—but persisting—enduring the five-thirty-a.m. practices and maintaining his academic focus enough to graduate from his prestigious private university with honors—and gain admission to a top law school.

And even during these first few months of law school where James had been willing to sacrifice nearly everything he really valued in life for more study time, swimming was the one exception. No matter what, James promised himself he would never give up his swim workouts, always making time for a daily four thousand yards in the university pool—even during exam week.

Swimming was one of the few things James could always count on to put life into perspective. It would always transport him to his own private universe where the annoying limitations of everyday life didn't apply, including even the limitation of gravity. It put him in a place that seemed, in a strange way, more real—a place where life made more sense somehow.

The ultimate bubble, perhaps.

No, he wouldn't give up his beloved swimming, and he wouldn't give up caring about the world either, James decided. Perhaps Chad was wrong. Perhaps James could have it all. Or, perhaps, Chad was right and he should drop out and find another career to pursue. James's future would depend upon how he did on his first exams. Only if he did exceptionally well would he stay. And he hoped, if he did end up succeeding in law school, that his personality wouldn't be incompatible with his future career in the bubble of the legal profession.

CHAPTER 2

THE ROAD NOT TAKEN

Four and a half years later, James sat at his desk in his small office at the firm contemplating the large stack of paperwork in front of him. The office, one of six in the middle, interior section of the firm's second floor, was windowless so he could never really know what was going on in the outside world or exactly what time it was without looking at his watch—but his inner clock told him it was around ten p.m. James looked at his watch. It was just before ten. He wouldn't be able to leave until at least two a.m. and would be lucky to catch five hours of sleep before getting up and repeating the same day over again. There were evenings James seriously considered just sleeping over at the office and forgetting about going home altogether.

But there was Sue to think about.

A quick coffee together before work hardly made for a marriage, but at least it was something.

Still, a part of James had grown to love life at the firm.

He liked the prestige of being a lawyer, the money was great, and James even enjoyed the challenging nature of the work, at least to a point.

And he was very good at what he did, according to Phil Blake, who had recently rewarded James with his own private office—a promotion from the shared offices of the other associates—and who hardly ever complimented anyone about the quality of their work at the firm—friend or not.

I should be happy, James thought.

It didn't help that finding the time to swim was impossible. He really missed it. And after nearly two years at the firm—sitting at his desk most of that time—James felt overweight and sluggish in a way he had never before experienced.

And James had a nagging feeling that his talents were going to waste—that he should be doing something more important with his life—something that would, in some small way, help change the world for the better.

And then there was his marriage.

It had been unfair to ask Sue to come to New York to be the wife of someone whose career would always come first in his life. He realized that now. He had understood the realities of working at a major law firm. Sue had not. It was his fault things weren't going well at home—and James was determined to make things better somehow.

As James contemplated his options, he thought about his wife of almost a year now—about the first time he had met Sue Ellen Bauer during his second year of law school. His first reaction to Sue had been that she wasn't his type—which had also been Sue's first impression of him, ironically—describing her new "excessively preppy" and "almost too young-looking" new boyfriend as "a Ken doll who had never been out of his box."

James wondered if their initial impressions of each other had been right after all.

Sue had grown up on her family's small farm in Idaho—an outdoor life betrayed by the clusters of freckles that dotted her always makeup-free nose and cheeks of her slightly weathered countenance. And a modest life hinted at by her complete lack of interest in fashion or style—her wardrobe a cobbled-together variety of hand-me-downs and functional no-name accessories and her hair—thick and dirty blond—always flying around her face in a frizzy mess as Sue had little inclination to do anything with it other than to occasionally and always unsuccessfully blow a tuft of it away from her dazzlingly blue eyes.

Sue had been an undergraduate when they met, finishing up her degree in environmental studies. And Sue was the product of her local public school—not some feeder school in a wealthy suburb that happened to be public—but a no-name, local public high school in the middle of nowhere Idaho, which helped make her refreshingly unpretentious—but which also meant that high-powered careers, fancy cars, and glamorous vacation houses weren't what Sue valued in life.

Even if he made partner someday, he wouldn't be able to make her happy, James lamented. He hated to admit it, but Phil Blake had been right about Sue after all. And now James faced a really awful choice.

Yes—he should have listened to Phil, the "voice of reason" in his life.

"She's not right for you, Hartman," Phil had admonished from the other side of his mahogany desk that fateful evening the previous January.

Although not one of the really fancy corner offices inhabited by the big rainmakers at the firm, Phil's office was a decent trophy for all the years of work Phil had put into his career, James had always thought—nice but always somewhat messy with folders piled up here and there—the office of a hard worker and a talented litigator.

James usually looked forward to his regular evening visits to Phil's office when the two decided to take a break from the grind and "shoot the bull."

But not that evening.

"She's not going to understand. A woman who marries someone who has a real chance to make partner here… She needs to understand… to have a clue… as to the kind of sacrifice…"

James sat silently that evening the previous January, confused and uncomfortable with Phil's stern "talk" about his personal life.

"Trust me, James. It won't work out, and best-case scenario you're distracted with a divorce early in your career..."

As Phil went on and James pretended to listen, his gaze turned toward the lonely framed photograph—partially hidden behind piles of legal folders—of Phil's wife and two daughters, ages five and seven in the picture but now several years older. James wondered how long it had been since Phil had spent quality time with any of them.

"The bottom line is... Sue is a traditional woman with small-town values who wants a traditional family and a normal life... And you can't give her that—not the way she envisions it. And you won't be happy either—believe me—I know you."

There had been an awkward pause as Phil leaned back in his chair, studying James as he composed his thoughts.

"I think you are going to be faced with making a choice—between her and here. Between being one of us... or having just an ordinary life. And I think you are going to make... I'm afraid you are going to make the wrong choice."

James hadn't wanted to admit to himself that he would ever need to make that choice.

At first there had been much reassuring to Sue—and to himself—that life would get better one day if they gave it time. But as the weeks and months wore on—as the grueling hours at the firm meant James and Sue saw less and less of each other—Sue began to question whether they would ever have the time to have a family together in a meaningful way and, more subtly, whether James was becoming a different person than the one she had fallen in love with.

And James began to question what type of person he was as well. Was he really the type of person Phil Blake believed him to be?

Phil's reaction to James's letter of resignation, however, was rather unexpected.

"I'm going to consider this a leave of absence."

James was stunned by Phil Blake's words. James knew that people didn't just take time off from the law. If they left, they almost always left for good.

"I know you, Hartman. You're one of us—and you're going to want to come back. Keep in touch, and when you learn that I'm right about you, give me a call."

And with that, James was out.

James's life at that moment reminded him of his favorite poem by Robert Frost—"The Road Not Taken"—in which a traveler comes to two roads which diverge and must choose between them. The two divergent paths symbolize decisions made in life, and because the end of the road is not visible, it is only *after* the journey is complete that the right choice—or mistake—becomes clear.

And because life's paths continually diverge, it is unlikely that a person can ever go back to that fork in the road and make the other choice—so the consequences of such decisions are almost always permanent.

James understood Frost's poem in a very personal way that day. And he understood that the road he had chosen was *the one less traveled by*—a road at the end of which he hoped he would find happiness.

CHAPTER 3

THE INTERVIEW

James sat across from Deborah Gerwitz, a woman in her midfifties, perhaps, with graying, dark blond shoulder-length hair with a professional yet slightly disheveled look, which gave James the impression she was used to dressing more casually.

James felt overdressed in his three-thousand-dollar suit.

They sat in a classroom in a public school, slightly too close to one another—no desk between them—Mrs. Gerwitz busily scribbling notes on a yellow pad as James described his reasons for wanting to be a part of the New York City Teaching Fellows program.

The questions were the typical ones one might be asked during an interview, and James couldn't help but think Mrs. Gerwitz was ticking them off a prepared list somewhere in her head or perhaps on her yellow pad. She didn't seem entirely comfortable in her role as interviewer, and James guessed she wasn't very experienced at it.

James described his reasons for wanting to teach. Although he didn't go into as much detail with Mrs. Gerwitz, both he and Sue had thought that teaching would be a logical choice for James. He already had an advanced degree and had good presentational skills—but more importantly, James had academic talent and a love of learning that he could surely impart to his students.

And while they had fleetingly considered other options for James within the legal profession, the whole point of leaving the firm was time—and the law was a profession that was measured in billable hours.

For James, inequality in public education was a legal issue that genuinely interested him—so much so that he had written a paper on the subject during his third year of law school. He had always thought it was both unjust and damaging to society that there were such vast differences in the quality of public schools from state to state and from neighborhood to neighborhood and had argued that a basic education should be considered a civil right in a modern society as it was nearly impossible to pursue happiness or maintain a true sense of liberty without one.

The Teaching Fellows program attempted to remedy such educational disparities in New York City by recruiting highly qualified people, many with real-world professional experience, to teach in public schools with the greatest need—and this appealed to James. Indeed, the opportunity to help reduce these disparities was the major reason James had rejected the easier idea of teaching at a private school.

The program also had the practical appeal of offering a free master's degree in education, and James presumed that he would receive, through that program, the majority of the training as well as the paper credentials he would need to succeed in the profession.

And then there was the time.

Sue's position at a not-for-profit environmental organization offered a good degree of flexibility—so she and James would have, in addition to traditional holidays, the summers together. And the prospect of spending summers with each other at first, and with their children in a few years' time, was a life plan they both looked forward to.

Mrs. Gerwitz had seemingly come to the end of her list of queries, and James was preparing to ask the obligatory questions one asks at the end of an interview to leave a good impression—when Mrs. Gerwitz abruptly stopped. She looked James over for a moment, taking a deep breath as she did.

It was an awkward pause.

She put down her yellow pad and continued in a different, more personal tone—as if starting the interview process over again from scratch—as if the compulsory questions were completed and the real questions could now be asked.

"James… here's the thing. I have no question you will find the academic requirements of this program to be easy. With your record… After law school—I suspect you will find them ridiculously easy, to be honest with you. There are a lot of applicants I have academic concerns about—not being able to handle the teacher exams—not being able to handle the job and the master's program at the same time… You are definitely not one of those."

James listened intently. The interview had veered sharply away from the standard and uninteresting one he had been participating in, and he realized he had severely underestimated Mrs. Gerwitz.

"Unfortunately, many of the applicants that I have to reject for academic reasons would have made excellent teachers for the kids this program is trying to help. I would have liked to have admitted them. But I can't admit them because I know they won't pass the teacher exams or be able to complete the master's program on time. And if they can't hack the academics, the system says they're out." Mrs. Gerwitz paused as she studied James with a slightly exasperated look on her face.

James was confused. He had been quite certain he would be admitted into the program—he had excellent credentials—but Mrs. Gerwitz seemed to have some serious doubts. She considered James for a moment more, then sighed as she leaned back in her chair.

"Don't get me wrong, James. You will almost certainly be admitted to this program—you're exactly what they're looking for." James relaxed a little as Mrs. Gerwitz continued. "You're actually one of the more qualified applicants we've had this year... on paper anyway."

James didn't quite know how to react, but Mrs. Gerwitz had not been anticipating a response and immediately launched into her first question.

"James... What would you do if you suspected that one of your students was mentally retarded?" Mrs. Gerwitz's intense eye contact with James was almost painful.

After a moment of shock that James was only partially successful in concealing, he attempted a thoughtful clarification of the question. "Well... I would have thought something like that would have been caught before high school," James stammered.

Mrs. Gerwitz nodded cynically. "Yes, that would seem logical. The system has had the student for ten or eleven years so you would think... But what would you do if you had a student in your class that you suspected was mentally retarded?" Mrs. Gerwitz retorted as she stared James down.

James wondered whether Mrs. Gerwitz's question was somehow rooted in her personal experience. Were things so bad in the public schools that he would really have to worry about something like this actually happening?

He tried again. "I think the first thing I'd do is consult with school officials and find out if the child had been eval—"

"And what if the school insists the child isn't mentally retarded, refuses to reevaluate the child, and tells you they must stay in your class?" Mrs. Gerwitz interrupted in a passionate, rapid-fire interrogation that seemed as if it had been asked many times but never answered to satisfaction by anyone over the years.

This is definitely personal, James thought as he considered what the next logical step might be. "Perhaps the child could be placed in a special education—"

"The parents haven't consented to that, and the child must stay in your class. What would you do?" Mrs. Gerwitz was stoic as she leaned in closer to scrutinize James.

James's professional instincts kicked in. He understood that his responsibility as a lawyer was to his clients—and as a teacher it would be to his students.

"Well… If that were my only option, then I would do the best I could for the student. I would probably try to tailor a curriculum especially for that student—possibly give them some different work they could handle— spend more time with the student, if possible… I would do what I could," James answered with a resigned exhalation.

"So you would accept that student as your responsibility then?" Mrs. Gerwitz probed in a more hopeful tone.

"Of course—if they were in my class, they would be my responsibility," James responded, maintaining sincere eye contact.

Mrs. Gerwitz, with a slight nod of her head, moved on to her next question. "Let's say your principal or your assistant principal required you to teach in a certain way—or made you teach certain material that you found to be ineffective. What would you do?"

This was an easier question for James as it was similar to a legal ethics hypothetical he had once studied, and he answered immediately. "The first thing I'd do is to investigate whether I was correct in my assessment of the material. I wouldn't assume that I knew more than my principal or my assistant principal—especially as a new teacher. I would try to teach the material in the way I was told—and if that wasn't working, I would try teaching the material in different ways—and if that didn't work, I would bring my concerns to my principal or assistant principal."

"And what if your superiors insisted that you teach this material or used this teaching method regardless of its effectiveness?" Mrs. Gerwitz queried with a note of exasperation in her voice.

James paused for a moment. Would school administrators really insist on teaching methods and materials that were ineffective?

"Ultimately, they're my kids and my responsibility—so I would have to teach them in another way that was effective," James answered with a shrug of his shoulders.

James's response succeeded in eliciting an almost imperceptible smile from Mrs. Gerwitz as she scribbled "my kids" and a few other notations on her yellow pad.

"What if your superiors found out you were doing things differently and threatened your career?" Mrs. Gertwitz inquired, looking up from her notes questioningly.

This time James didn't really have to think about his answer. "I would have to give the same answer. Ultimately, your responsibility is to your students."

Mrs. Gerwitz made a final note on her yellow pad and, after some obligatory concluding remarks, shook James's hand and wished him luck.

Afterward, James went swimming.

With time no longer a billable commodity, James could swim again and devote some of his energies to regaining the physique he had lost during his years of physical inactivity at the firm, investing in an expensive swim club membership at the best pool in the city.

It had been difficult at first—sets of hundreds that would have been a warm-up in years past were now a full workout that left James breathless and exhausted. But James had persisted, slowly adding yardage, daily sets of push-ups, and runs in the park with Sue when the weather was nice. He quickly dropped twenty-five pounds and felt better than he had in years.

And today as he swam, James felt especially strong as he felt the water rush by him like it used to back in college, passing swimmers in neighboring lanes as if they were standing still.

James was back.

James briefly wondered what he was getting himself into.

He knew there were problems in the system, but surely Mrs. Gerwitz had presented some extreme cases. Anyway, he was one of the better qualified candidates for the program—Mrs. Gerwitz had said so in the interview.

So James felt, as he swam his four-thousand-yard workout that afternoon, very confident about his future—and was looking forward to beginning a new chapter in his life.

CHAPTER 4

THE TEACHING FELLOWS PROGRAM AND RACE

Just prior to the start of the Teaching Fellows program, James and Sue moved from their high-priced rental on the East Side into their new, one-bedroom apartment on the Upper West Side near Columbia University—made possible by one last large gift from James's parents before his father would retire the following year.

It was far too small for Sue, who felt boxed in by most New York City apartments, and she worried about being able to afford the pricey mortgage and the maintenance on James's vastly reduced salary.

But James hadn't wanted to move farther uptown to Hudson Heights or to Brooklyn, extolling the virtues of his old neighborhood—and he had assured Sue, to her great skepticism, that "finances always work themselves out in the long run."

Still, James promised he would try to live on a much stricter budget, even reluctantly agreeing to cancel his expensive swim club membership and use the pool at the local YMCA instead.

The Teaching Fellows program began soon after the move at the beginning of the summer. Opening day ceremonies were mostly motivational speeches from politicians and other city bigwigs—the same praise and good wishes repeated from speaker to speaker that James quickly tuned out.

"This is your union, and we will fight for you!" the speaker shouted, pounding her fist on the lectern.

James was suddenly paying attention, focused on Randy Weingarten, head of the United Federation of Teachers. The tone of her speech was different—confrontational and far more personal than any of the others. And every other word she used was "fighting," it seemed.

James knew Randy Weingarten was an attorney who had used her skills to negotiate teachers' contracts on behalf of the UFT, and there was a litigious quality to her presentation that made James feel uncomfortable. As an attorney, James understood that litigation was messy—and almost always ended up costing both sides a lot of time and money—which was fine with the lawyers involved but often never really solved anything.

James had never been a member of a union. Although he could see how this would be to his personal advantage as unions fought for jobs and benefits for their membership, he had more difficulty seeing how this self-interest would benefit the students and the system—and wondered, as he listened to Randy Weingarten's increasingly combative-sounding presentation, whether some of what the teachers' union stood for might be part of the problem.

Indeed, the next speaker, another union representative, went out of his way to define public schools as "union shops," a description that evoked the image of factories whose assembly workers were teachers and whose products were students—a picture of education which struck James as highly unfitting.

After opening ceremonies concluded, the teaching fellows were separated into their different cohorts—groups of thirty or so who would train together during the summer. The cohorts were assigned to one of several schools where they would complete their summer fieldwork—after which they would become full-time teachers in the fall.

James and half his group were assigned to teach at Benjamin Harrison High School in the Bronx. Most of the other half were assigned to William Howard Taft High School, also in the Bronx—and had bragging rights as Taft had the reputation of being the very worst of the very worst high schools in the city, as well as having the curious distinction of graduating legendary film director Stanley Kubrick and possibly inspiring him, in part, to make *A Clockwork Orange*.

Meeting the members of his cohort was very reassuring to James. They were a surprisingly well-qualified group of people, he thought. Although there weren't any other attorneys, virtually all had a similar educational background to James with representatives from all the *US News and World Report's* top-ranked schools.

A few even had advanced degrees.

Among the very large group of teaching fellows assigned to Benjamin Harrison was Lauren Weiler, a recent Brown graduate and predictably quite liberal. Lauren was the most outgoing of the group and, judging by her strategically torn, bargain-basement clothing, from serious money, James guessed. Lauren had somehow gotten into a friendly but spirited debate with Gerald Houston about the merits—or lack thereof—of Ronald Regan's presidency.

Gerald, a University of Chicago graduate, was one of the few politically conservative people in the program—although he would argue that his brand of libertarianism actually made him more progressive than most. He was quietly intelligent, and his strategy debating Lauren was to nod at appropriate moments during Lauren's more emotionally charged arguments and then calmly and neatly point out their flaws in a concise sentence or two—which would leave Lauren frantically searching for more words to throw at Gerald—which she would somehow always find—and the debate would continue as before.

There was Jan Walker who was an English major at Swarthmore and had been in publishing for a short time and hated it; Jane Sherwin, a native New Yorker who had been in public relations for four years and was an English major at the University of Pennsylvania and whose older brother had been a high school classmate of James's; Andy Stine who had gone to Amherst and who had been an editor for five years; and Robert Sullivan, an always jovial and very stout former wrestler who was sorry he hadn't majored in history instead of English at Yale but had done so mainly because of his interest in theatre—and was looking forward to putting his acting skills to use in the classroom.

James and Robert quickly discovered their mutual interest in politics as well as their shared disappointment that the board of education wouldn't let them teach history instead of English due to their undergraduate majors.

There were many others in the cohort, more than thirty in all, with similar backgrounds and stories. The majority of the group's reasons for wanting to teach were similar to James's: dissatisfaction with their careers, the desire to do something meaningful with their lives, and the desire, on a personal level, to have more time.

James was excited to work with such a talented group of people and felt very much at home that day as he and the others in his cohort discovered how much they all had in common. Indeed, pretty much everyone James met was from his world more or less.

Pretty much everyone—except for one guy.

The one guy was Martin King, assigned with James to Benjamin Harrison and who would be asked by his students whether his middle name was "Luther" more times than one would have believed possible that summer.

But Martin would always reply with a grin that his middle name was actually "Monty" after Monty Hall of *Let's Make a Deal* fame because his mother had been such a die-hard fan of the show back in the day and she just couldn't help herself. The kids always got a laugh out of the story—and Martin quickly became their favorite teacher.

Martin, or Mr. Monty as he would later be called, was one of the younger participants in the Teaching Fellows program. He was a recent graduate—but not from the same pedigree of college or university that James or any of the other teaching fellows James met that day had attended.

And unlike the rest of the cohort, Martin had never really been a full-time student. Instead, he had gone to one of the city's community colleges for two years and then transferred to a four-year city college, eventually cobbling together his BA in five and a half years by taking mostly night classes year-round while working days managing a Modells.

The other difference between Martin and the rest of the cohort was that Martin Monty King was Black.

It hadn't occurred to James that day, but the vast majority of the participants in the Teaching Fellows program were White.

James had been brought up not to think about the importance of race all that much—a good thing in that James, and many others who grew up in similar circumstances, truly believed that race was unimportant, that racial divisions could be eliminated in time, and that much progress had been made toward that goal.

Unfortunately, living in such an idealistic bubble had also caused James and many of the other teaching fellows to believe that the rest of the world was actually that far along in its perception of race. And it wasn't long into the summer before they would be shocked and dismayed by the reality of how deeply race divided New York City's public school system.

The vast majority of teachers in the system were White, while the racial makeup of their students was diametrically opposed—with most either Black or Hispanic. And the public schools were, themselves, divided along racial lines—either by catchment—students in poor neighborhoods and affluent neighborhoods were usually required to attend their catchment school—or by selectivity, where the top public schools accepted students on the basis of a standardized test that required expensive tutoring poorer kids couldn't afford. Students at those selective high schools were mostly White and Asian.

The students at nonselective Benjamin Harrison High School, by contrast, were almost entirely Black or Hispanic.

James understood these statistics represented a vicious cycle—that their causes were many and solutions were far from clear. What was very clear to James was that Martin King's success with his students demonstrated again and again the importance of role models in motivating students to aspire to do well in school.

And it wasn't just that Martin was African American.

Martin was from the same world as his students—growing up poor in an often dangerous neighborhood, raised by a single mother who had the fortitude to make sure her son got an education in spite of the system, and instilling in him the value of a college education as a way to move up in the world.

Martin knew the world those kids came from. He spoke their language, and he genuinely cared about improving their lives—and the kids were drawn to him. They looked up to him. They were inspired by him.

It also didn't hurt that Martin was, by far, the most talented of the teaching fellows at Benjamin Harrison that summer. He was incredibly charismatic, his lessons were creative, and most of all, he was born to work with kids. And whenever James and the others in his cohort had the chance to watch Martin's magic in the classroom, they were taught the somewhat painful lesson that most of what made a great teacher great just wasn't teachable.

But the Teaching Fellows program would try that summer, through fieldwork and through classroom instruction, to teach the cohort how to be great teachers anyway.

The cohort quickly bonded, and new and close friendships were made. The group considered themselves a team, and there was talk—over many drinks and usually led by Lauren Weiler—of "taking over" Benjamin Harrison—that there were so many of them that they could, together, have a real impact on the school—that they could really make a difference.

James watched the others laughing and drinking at their local watering hole one Friday evening early that summer as he nursed his barely touched beer with a faint smile on his face. He allowed himself to fantasize about a future Benjamin Harrison High School with the teaching fellows in charge. The bad teachers would be forced out, and the school would return to its former glory with a dedicated faculty and high standards that would be an inspiration to change other schools and eventually the entire system. And when that happened, the children of poor families would be given the same opportunities as the children of the rich, and the world would be changed. He and the others would have the satisfaction of seeing their former students graduating from their prestigious alma maters and knowing that they had put their expensive education to good use by giving back.

Okay, perhaps he was being a little optimistic, James reflected. *Drinking the Kool-Aid if not the beer,* he chuckled to himself. But James was excited at the prospect of doing something important with his life—of actually helping, in a small way, to change the world for the better.

CHAPTER 5

SUMMER SCHOOL

Summer school for the teaching fellows came in two flavors.

They would attend summer school at City College for the beginning of the Master's Program in Education, along with a series of special training seminars outside the master's program, which covered everything from preparing for the Liberal Arts and Sciences Test (LAST) teacher exam to classroom management, and they would be assistant teachers in summer school classes at Benjamin Harrison High School in the Bronx.

The days started early, traveling to the Bronx to student teach during the first half of the day, and ended in the evening after the group attended classes or training seminars. For the majority of the cohort, the days were long—but not for James. James was used to working into the early hours of the morning at the firm, and for him, getting home in time for a late dinner with Sue and to bed at a reasonable hour—not to mention having most weekends free—was an absolute luxury.

As the weekends approached, large sections of the group would often meet up for much-welcomed drinks—always convivial events that included spouses, significant others, and the stray friend or two—and nearly always incorporated a spirited debate or two between Lauren Weiler and her always reliable opponent Gerald Houston.

For James, the level of informal social interaction with his new colleagues took some getting used to, considering the formal nature socializing usually took at the firm. And it didn't help that James wasn't much of a drinker.

But spending time with the group and, in particular, with Sue, who seemed to naturally relate to everyone in the cohort, always put a smile on James's face and allowed him to loosen up in both his dress and comportment in a way he hadn't in many years.

Adding to James's feelings of complacency was the unchallenging nature of the master's program. In truth, it wasn't long before James and most of the others looked upon the master's program as something of a joke—more of an academic hoop to jump through than a resource that would actually help them with their teaching.

They would spend their afternoons analyzing classic stories and plays that most had already read in high school and on a level that nearly all considered simplistic. They had been English-related majors at the nation's best colleges and universities, after all.

The lessons in teaching and education were equally useless—mostly a repeat of concepts learned by anyone who had taken an introductory-level psychology course—and always combined with the seemingly common-sense notion that students were "hungry to learn" if teachers provided them with an exciting and supportive environment.

Rarely did the coursework offer anything of practical value.

James was just thankful the coursework was easy so he could focus on his student teaching at Benjamin Harrison High School—a place where he would actually learn something that summer.

The high school was a very large building dating back to 1919 that retained much of its original architecture. It was an impressive facility with plenty of resources. Although needing some renovation and fresh paint in places, the school seemed even grander during the summer months when comparatively few students graced its majestic halls and occupied its large-windowed classrooms.

Benjamin Harrison was also a "scanning school," which meant that students had to pass through metal detectors in order to gain admittance. Why some schools were chosen to be scanning schools and others weren't, and how those decisions were made, was an issue that James would later spend considerable time pondering.

But for the moment, James simply considered the metal detectors an oddity as he had plenty of other issues to think about—like his first teaching assignment—an English class where he had been assigned to work with thirty-nine-year veteran teacher, Mrs. Barbara Lemmons.

James was excited to try teaching for the first time but was even more elated to be paired with his new friend Robert Sullivan to be co-assistant teachers in the same classroom that summer.

And after meeting the elderly Barbara Lemmons, both immediately realized they had been given a valuable opportunity. They would be able to experiment with different types of lesson plans and teaching styles—hone their skills for the fall—and have the chance to pretty much run an entire classroom that summer.

This was because Barbara Lemmons was insane.

At least that was Robert's assessment. James agreed that she had to be suffering from some sort of mental illness but disagreed that she was actually insane—at least most of the time.

Whether poor silver-haired Mrs. Lemmons had suffered some sort of a nervous breakdown from her many years of teaching—a frightening notion considering the career path the two were embarking upon—or was the victim of early dementia, became a daily debate between the two that would have both James and Robert periodically switching sides with each bizarre lesson they watched Mrs. Lemmons attempt to teach.

On a good day, her classes would actually start off well but would soon drift into the incomprehensible. Robert was always pretending to sneeze or cough to cover his mouth to keep from bursting into raucous laughter, occasionally eliciting a tissue or a lozenge from Mrs. Lemmons, who was completely oblivious and all too happy to pause the class while she rummaged through her purse to find whatever therapy was needed for her sickly student teacher.

James sometimes pretended to work on his lesson plans as an excuse to look away.

It was clear to James that Mrs. Lemmons had been a good teacher once. There were actually flashes of brilliance in her lessons from time to time, but they would quickly devolve into gibberish—at which point James or Robert would politely offer a comment or question to nudge Mrs. Lemmons back on track—or simply take over the class altogether, which was more often the case.

And Mrs. Lemmons was always happy to cede the class over to James or Robert so she could read her newspaper or work on her cross-word puzzles.

Much of the first day, however, was consumed with taking attendance.

James had been looking forward to some sort of introductory class— students and teachers introducing themselves in a fun and creative way— some sort of writing assessment perhaps.

None of it happened.

Attendance wasn't something James had really thought about. He knew it had been silently taken at his private high school during the first minute or two of class, but the process was largely invisible. Attendance in public school was, apparently, a much more important affair.

It involved cumbersome, multilayered bubble sheets—and little cards to go with them—that had to be filled in every day and would eventually drive James slightly crazy. Perhaps the unwieldy process had contributed to Mrs. Lemmons's insanity as well, because even with the small group of less than twenty students that had shown up to take her class that summer, Mrs. Lemmons was hardly up to the challenge of taking attendance.

In addition to her general bewilderment and difficulty pronouncing many of the names on the list, let alone attaching them to the young faces staring back at her with gazes that were rapidly losing interest, Mrs. Lemmons had rather poor eyesight and couldn't see well enough to match the correct bubble with the correct name.

This was problematic because the layered bubble sheets were designed to make copies, so each mistake was repeated in triplicate. Needless to say, James and Robert took over attendance after the first day, and classes from then on were much improved.

So went James's first day of teaching.

With few exceptions, the others in the cohort had negative comments about the quality of the teachers they had been assigned to, although Mrs. Lemmons quickly garnered the prize for being the least competent—especially after Robert perfected an impression of her that he was all too happy to perform after a couple of beers to an inappropriately raucous group of teaching fellows.

Teaching, it turned out, was relatively easy.

The inexperienced group of teaching fellows was better by far than the vast majority of veteran teachers at Benjamin Harrison that summer.

The master's program was a joke.

So it wasn't surprising that the general feeling of optimism intensified as the summer portion of the program progressed.

And for the moment, the challenge James and the others were mostly focused on wasn't their teaching but the first academic hoop the group would have to jump through—the teacher exam known as the LAST.

CHAPTER 6

THE WARNINGS, THE MUPPETS, AND THE LAST

The Teaching Fellows program had been pushing review for the Liberal Arts and Sciences Test (LAST) since the very start of the program. The LAST was a general knowledge test that was required for teacher certification, and the cohort had two opportunities to pass the LAST before the end of the summer.

Failure to pass the LAST meant you couldn't be certified by the state and were, therefore, out of the program. So the cohort was presented with review seminars and study materials for the LAST at every opportunity.

This seemed like overkill to James.

James had, early on, taken a single practice LAST, which he had finished in less than half the allotted time with a nearly perfect score, during which he uttered the phrase "This is such bullshit" to Sue exactly eighteen times.

Needless to say, James made the decision that he didn't need to study for the LAST—as did most of the cohort. This was because James and the others who had grown up under similar circumstances were well acquainted with standardized tests and had learned, through years of prep courses and expensive private tutoring, the tricks and strategies of how to do well on those types of assessments long ago.

James would attend the required training sessions but would always bring along some work to do so the time would be productive.

Predictably the LAST, which took place at the Javits Center early in the summer, became yet another object of ridicule for James and his cohort. As with all standardized tests, a few simple strategies could be used to eliminate most of the wrong choices.

And the essay question had been particularly well suited for James as it involved the rights of journalists to maintain the confidentiality of their sources from prosecutors—a legal rights issue James was able to fully dissect in a creatively written essay he was actually quite proud of.

With the LAST out of the way and its passage a done deal, James was able to focus on teaching. His first lesson—a class on basic essay writing—was well organized. Robert gave James's lesson plan an A plus, but the delivery was a bit mechanical according to Robert.

"Don't be afraid to be yourself up there. It isn't just about saying the lines, you know."

"I guess good teaching really is one-fourth perspiration and three-fourths theatre," James said to Robert as he bowed and tipped his imaginary hat in admiration of Robert's particularly entertaining lesson using a short story about cheating called *Arnie's Test Day* where Robert had his students, to their great amusement, enthusiastically debating the merits of cheating in school and describing several clever cheating techniques not mentioned in the story that James made a mental note to look out for in future classes.

As it turned out, it was a great advantage for James to have Robert as an audience during his crucial first teaching experience.

While James had a lot of personality compared with many of his former colleagues at the firm, that wasn't saying much. And Robert, with his theatre background and comedic flair, was able over the course of the summer to help James develop a more relaxed teaching style that better connected with his young audience—and even helped him inject some much-needed humor into his classes.

But Robert and James would both learn from watching the star of the cohort—Mr. "Monty" Martin King. One particular lesson the two were able to watch had his class performing a modern rap version of *Romeo and Juliet* where the rival families were from rival street gangs. Neither James nor Robert had ever seen students so engaged.

"So… How long before we learn to teach a class like that?" James turned to ask Robert as sarcastically as he was able.

"Never. You will never learn to teach a class like that." Robert paused as he pondered their situation. "And neither will I. We're smart. We're good people. We'll be decent teachers someday. Martin's a great teacher."

With Robert's help and daily practice, James's teaching, though not Martin King awe-inspiring, continued to steadily improve over the summer. The small group of twenty students had dwindled to around fifteen, which allowed James and Robert the time to give each student some much-needed individual attention.

It had been immediately apparent to James, after looking at their written work, that these kids hadn't been taught how to write—or encouraged to think critically—although interestingly, many had somehow been taught really good penmanship.

Indeed, the quality of the handwriting displayed by many of the students made James more than a little self-conscious, as he had inherited the professional scrawl most common among doctors—the type only pharmacists seem able to decipher—and it was an effort for him to develop a non-cursive style for the blackboard that could be written quickly enough for use in a live class while still remaining legible more or less.

Although penmanship and neatness generally wasn't an issue with James's first group of students, the actual content was. It was as if the students had designed their papers to be looked at but not actually read.

Grammar and spelling were, all too often, seemingly considered optional—but more disturbingly the work displayed a lack of critical thinking and analysis that was replaced by summary and repetition—usually in a disorganized mess that ended whenever the required page count had been reached.

As bad as their writing often was, and as far behind as many of these students were, it was amazing what could be achieved with a little one-on-one attention—and this led to James's first small success as a teacher.

Javier Ramos was an engaging fourteen-year-old, with an always smiling round face, and a die-hard New York Yankees fan and who had made the mistake of forgetting to take off his New York Yankees baseball cap—a nearly permanent fixture atop Javier's overly rounded cranium—on the first day of class.

Although Mrs. Lemmons couldn't remember names or take attendance and was mostly disengaged from her role as a teacher and was generally oblivious, she did remember the rules—and the sight of a hat atop Javier's head triggered a Pavlovian response in the veteran teacher of yelling and screaming in English and broken Spanish.

"Your hat! Your hat! *Tú sombrero!*" Mrs. Lemmons yelled at the top of her lungs, her face quickly reddening.

"Sorry...," Javier responded, reflexively removing his hat as he avoided eye contact with Mrs. Lemmons.

"*Cállate!* Sit down!" Mrs. Lemmons commanded, pointing to a lonely desk at the end of the first row.

The poor boy was sent scurrying to his seat, clutching his prized Yankees cap in both hands. Mrs. Lemmons coldly stared him down before going back to her crossword puzzle.

James cringed.

Javier's ever-present smile was gone as he looked around for a safe place to put his precious piece of New York Yankees memorabilia.

It was obvious to James that Javier hadn't meant any disrespect. The kid just wore the cap everywhere and had forgotten—and now he was trying to figure out someplace safe to put his treasured headgear where he wouldn't have another memory lapse and forget to take it with him when class was over.

"I could look after it for you if you'd like," James offered.

"Thanks, mister," Javier said, looking up at James as his smile slowly returned to his round face.

Although James was only a casual baseball fan, he made it his business over the summer to reacquaint himself with the game so that he could keep up with Javier in a conversation about the New York Yankees, which was practically all Javier ever talked about.

And it was through this interest and the trust he had developed with Javier from that first day that James was able to help greatly improve Javier's writing ability.

James had recently taught a class on the essay-writing process in an attempt to eliminate repetition and introduce some much-needed organization into the papers he had read that summer. Although there was a part of James that considered the lesson to be ridiculously elementary, they needed to be shown a basic writing process. This was something that should have been taught in grade school rather than in high school. He understood that the class needed the lesson, whether it was a review of something they had forgotten or whether it was something they had never been taught.

So James reviewed the basics of brainstorming and outlining, the elements of a good introduction, what constituted a good thesis, supporting body paragraphs, and so on—comparing a good essay to a good sandwich with the introduction and the conclusion being the two halves of a Kaiser roll.

"What's a Kaiser roll, mister?" one of his young students asked with complete sincerity.

Apart from the long and spirited debate as to exactly what a Kaiser roll was, the lesson seemed to go over well with the class, and James had the students write an essay on a subject that interested them and would be outlined in class and completed at home.

Almost immediately Javier's smile left him—replaced with a frustrated stare down at a blank sheet of paper. James went over to help.

"I don't know what to write about, mister." Javier moaned, shaking his head.

"Why don't you write about something you know a lot about—the Yankees, for example?"

"I can write about the Yankees?" Javier looked up from his blank paper.

"Sure. I kind of expected that you *would* write about the Yankees."

Javier paused and thought for a moment.

"But what about the Yankees should I write about?" Javier asked with a somber expression.

"That's a good question. You need to narrow down your topic so your essay won't be too general. How about writing an essay about your favorite player? Who's your favorite player, Javier?"

"Well… who's my favorite player or who's my favorite Yankee? Because my favorite player of all time wasn't a Yankee."

James was visibly surprised. Even support for players on the New York Mets was considered sacrilegious in Javier's book.

"My favorite player of all time is Roberto Clemente," Javier declared as his infectious smile returned.

James had heard of Roberto Clemente, of course.

But as Javier eagerly educated James about the baseball sensation that played for the Pittsburgh Pirates decades before Javier was even born, James understood that Roberto Clemente was a hero to him and many others—not just because of his howitzer of a throwing arm, his record twelve golden gloves, or his three thousand hits, but because he was a person who had endured years of racial prejudice in a segregated America and had died in a plane crash trying to deliver aid to the victims of an earthquake in Nicaragua.

"Most people don't know that about him—they just know he played baseball and that there's a school named after him," Javier lamented.

James worked with Javier for the rest of the class brainstorming and outlining a very decent essay on Roberto Clemente, and James reminded the class to complete their essays for homework.

"You know, mister—that wasn't so hard," Javier proclaimed, his smile restored.

"It really isn't that hard once you get the hang of it. So Javier… Do you think everyone will actually write the paper for homework, or is this going to be like my Muppets quiz?"

Javier's smile widened into a guilty chuckle.

The infamous Muppets quiz was James's first attempt at composing an assessment. It was a short vocabulary quiz on words collected over several weeks, and James had decided to make it easy. He had made the quiz multiple choice with a correct answer, an opposite definition, and a third choice of "Muppets" just for fun.

To James's astonishment, nearly every student in the class failed the quiz, choosing "Muppets" as the correct definition for words such as "flourish," "aspire," and "analogy"—with many, including Javier, guessing the "Muppets" option over and over again. The lesson here wasn't for the students—it was for James—who learned that getting his students to study was going to be more difficult than just giving them an assignment.

"No, mister. I think they'll do it—most of them anyway. It's something they gotta hand in. It ain't like it's a quiz where they can guess."

"Isn't," James corrected.

"That's right, mister. It ain't like it's a quiz."

It was usual at the end of class for students and teachers to go their separate ways, but on this day, Javier tagged along at James's side.

"Hey, mister. You gonna teach here in the fall?"

"Yes. All of us are. Me, Robert… I mean, Mr. Sullivan. There are a lot of us. We're part of the Teaching Fellows program."

"Oh… Well you seem like a good guy—so let me give you a few tips on what you gotta do to succeed here."

James felt Javier's hand suddenly on his shoulder as the two stopped to face one another in the middle of the hallway.

The personal contact was a bit too familiar for James, but this was going to be personal advice that Javier wouldn't give to just anybody—and James appreciated the gesture. And James also appreciated the seriousness of the expression which now graced Javier's normally jovial round face—a seriousness he had never before seen in his young student, who was now looking him square in the eye with complete earnestness.

"First, you gotta be mad strict. And you gotta be mean. And you gotta set rules. And when the kids they break the rules, you gotta come down hard. You gotta understand—ain't nobody here in the summer. When school really start, this place a zoo, yo."

Javier studied James's confused expression, took a deep breath, and tried again.

"These kids ain't like you be—they ain't gonna respect nice. Me, I know different. Some of the others too. But to most of them, nice is weak—something you take advantage of. You be nice to them, they walk all over you. So you be tough. Be mad strict and be tough and you'll do okay."

James, after taking a moment to digest Javier's thoughtful counsel and decipher some of the unfamiliar slang, thanked Javier for his advice, assuring him he would keep it in mind, and left, slightly bewildered, for his afternoon class at City College—which coincidently happened to be about classroom management.

Needless to say, the academic version of classroom management differed markedly from Javier's version.

The general philosophy was that some rules were, of course, required—but to maintain the supportive classroom atmosphere, rules shouldn't be imposed upon the class. Rather, they should be in the form of a contract between the teacher and their students.

It was a fun class, with James and the other teaching fellows drawing up class contracts and reading them aloud. The more progressive the contract, the more applause it received—which made sense from the perspective of someone coming from James's world.

He and the others had attended, for the most part, progressive schools with small classes of highly motivated students who thrived in an informal environment with few rules where students often addressed teachers by their first names.

James with his legal background had the best lesson—combining a review of basic contract law with a tutorial on negotiation where students and teacher would negotiate the terms of the agreement, which would later be professionally printed and on display in the classroom—signed by every student and the teacher.

Everyone loved the lesson—but James couldn't help but think, as he received an ovation from the class that day, about Javier's advice—really more of a warning—that the picture being painted by academia—and what seemed like common sense to James and the others—wasn't the same picture of school that Javier and many of his classmates at Benjamin Harrison and similar schools were seeing.

And James, in the very back of his mind, wondered if something as reasonable sounding as a negotiated contract would be as effective in the reality Javier had described as it sounded in theory.

There would be one more warning for James and the others about the reality that was to come in the form of a special seminar on classroom management that was not part of the master's curriculum. Special seminars were held from time to time by the Teaching Fellows program and were usually headed by working teachers or administrators to supplement the master's program with more practical information.

This particular seminar was conducted, in part, by Mr. Joseph Biles, a twenty-five-plus-year mathematics teacher who had spent his entire career in high schools similar to Benjamin Harrison in both Brooklyn and the Bronx.

The word that first came to James's mind to describe Mr. Biles was "grizzled." He looked as if he were a man in his sixties on the verge of keeling over from a heart attack brought on by many years of a stress-filled career and the large protruding belly that such careers often feed—but he could have been a wreck of a man in his forties for all James could tell.

And his general manner matched his disheveled appearance, garnering him the almost instant disapproval of the entire cohort of teaching fellows—Lauren Weiler whispering just a little too loudly something about Joseph Biles being "part of the problem."

And it didn't help that the purpose of the seminar was to learn more about classroom management—something Mr. Biles apparently considered himself an expert in. He began in a gruff voice with a heavy Brooklyn accent and in a slightly cynical tone with a blunt question.

"So… What are your rules going to be and how are you going to enforce those rules? How are you going make your students respect your authority?" Mr. Biles scanned over his audience, taking in their shocked expressions with a faint smirk that graced his pockmarked, poorly shaven face.

There was a murmur of disapproval—not as much because of the content of the question but because of the way in which it was asked—with a note of confrontation and a tone of superiority—as if Mr. Biles expected a quarrel with what he considered to be a naive audience of pampered upper-class Ivy League idealists that he fully expected to disagree with his methods.

With an almost imperceptible leer, he continued. "Seating assignments on the first day of class. Great rule. You take every kid who sat down in the back of the room and make them sit in the front. You spot kids you think are friends—they sit on opposite sides of the room. And don't be shy about changing the seating assignments—I do it a couple of times a semester, just because."

James looked over at Lauren, who had an expression of absolute disgust on her face. James knew she couldn't keep silent for much longer.

"Dress code. Unfortunately, we can't do much about that—we don't require uniforms in New York City public schools—although we should. But we do have rules against hats and do-rags, and you can establish your authority that way," Mr. Biles lectured, as he paced the length of the small stage with authority.

Hats again, James thought as he rolled his eyes.

"What is your rule on late assignments? You don't accept them—period. If they don't hand in an assignment on time, they fail. If they didn't follow the instructions for the assignment—they fail. Now... As new teachers, you probably won't be allowed to fail an entire class—and that's a problem. So you'll have to be selective. But once they give you tenure..."

Lauren couldn't contain herself any longer and stood up from her seat. "Excuse me, sir, but isn't what you're telling us to do really part of the problem? Aren't all these arbitrary rules and regulations... and your general attitude, quite frankly, the reason these kids hate school?"

There was scattered applause. Joseph Biles responded with a condescending chuckle.

Lauren continued undaunted. "One of the reasons I've had a good experience—and I think all of us have had good experiences in school—is that we've had friendly, supportive teachers in an environment where we were free..."

"Look, Miss...?"

"Weiler."

"Look, Miss Weiler. I'm just telling you what you're going to need to do to survive..."

"But I'm not here… None of us are here to just 'survive'—I'm here—we're here—to try to change things so that these kids…" Lauren stammered, nearly in tears.

"And I'm just telling you what you're going to have to do to survive in a school like… Where are you going to teach in the fall?"

"Benjamin Harrison."

Joseph Biles burst into loud, feigned laughter. "You want to teach a class at Benjamin Harrison with no rules? Good luck, lady!"

Lauren, stunned into temporary silence, would have erupted into an emotional tirade she would have later regretted if it weren't for her reliable debate partner, Gerald Houston, who came to her rescue with a characteristically thoughtful question.

"What do you think about class contracts? One of the techniques we learned in our master's program for creating a set of mutually agreed-upon rules was to create a class contract during the first day that the teacher and the students can negotiate together and sign."

A look of skepticism graced Mr. Biles's face as he weighed his response. "Oh yeah. I've heard of that. Never tried it. I don't think it would work—but it couldn't hurt, I suppose."

Lauren seemed to have found some more words to throw at Mr. Biles and was about to continue her argument, but Joseph Biles beat her to it, proving that he did, indeed, know how to control a classroom.

"Look, Miss Weiler—I understand what you're saying. And you might get lucky and get a good class now and again—even at a place like Benjamin Harrison. And then you can relax a bit. But think of it as tough love. If you lose your class because you aren't strong enough from day one, you will never get them back, and then you aren't going to help anybody. You aren't going to help them—and you certainly aren't going to help yourself."

The rest of the week was dominated by conversations about Joseph Biles and the dictatorial classroom management techniques he so strongly advocated. Lauren Weiler was particularly incensed, and couldn't understand why Mr. Biles was even a teacher.

"He hates those kids," she kept insisting.

James wasn't so sure. It was hard for him to see how Joseph Biles could be a good teacher. He didn't seem particularly empathetic or creative—or even all that bright. He may very well have been some hack who was hanging around for the health insurance and a fatter pension. Or he may have been an effective teacher. James would never know for sure.

James wondered if, perhaps, Joseph Biles was just trying to be honest—trying to be one of the few people involved with the Teaching Fellows program who wasn't shy about telling the cohort the truth that summer.

The issues of Joseph Biles and classroom management would soon be forgotten, however, as a much more serious crisis was about to hit the cohort. James received his LAST score in the mail. It was nearly perfect as he expected it would be, with a perfect score on the essay, which was unusual even for the academically talented group of teaching fellows.

And the results were pretty much the same for everybody else—except for one guy. The news quickly filtered down among the shocked members of the cohort that their most talented member, Martin Monty King, had failed the LAST.

CHAPTER 7

BETRAYAL AND LOSS

Lauren Weiler, James, and a few of the others in the cohort offered to tutor Martin for his second and last chance to pass the LAST so he could stay in the program. However, Lauren's reliably positive attitude turned uncharacteristically pessimistic after just one session.

"He just hasn't had very much experience with standardized tests," Lauren said, shaking her head as she dropped off some prep materials with James.

James was surprised that Lauren had given up on Martin so easily and was very confident going into his first tutoring session with Martin that he would be able to do a much better job. James had, after all, negotiated the most standardized tests of anyone in the group, including the bar exam.

It would be relatively easy to teach Martin—an obviously intelligent and talented guy—a process of elimination strategy which would give him a good chance of passing. But after reviewing a sample question involving the interpretation of the poem "Child of the Americas" with Martin, all James could feel was some of Martin's confusion and frustration with the newest and seemingly insurmountable obstacle in his life—the standardized test known as the LAST.

"The answer they want is too simplistic." Martin was adamant.

"I know. But you can eliminate these two and it's the best remaining choice…"

"I disagree. Yes—it's literally true that 'a person's identity can comprise many cultures and languages.' Choice *D*. I mean, that's obvious," Martin countered with a scowl.

"But the answer you chose—choice *A*—talks about 'retaining a strong sense of ethnic identity' as being 'an empowering response to discrimination'—and the poem doesn't really talk about…"

"It doesn't have to," Martin insisted.

"But if the poem doesn't talk about discrimination…"

"Doesn't it matter who's reading the poem as to how it is interpreted?" Martin squirmed in his chair. "Look, James. I don't mean anything by this, but I don't think you can relate to this poem in the same way that I can."

James suddenly felt very awkward in his role as teacher as it was evident to him that not only was Martin right but that Martin had given "Child of the Americas" a great deal more thought than he had.

"I mean… For example, James… I was almost late to school this morning because I missed my bus and I couldn't hail a cab. I get stopped by the police constantly. I get looked at differently in stores, elevators… You name it. In America, if you're a member of a minority group, you're put into a category and discriminated against all the time. That's my normal. So I have a choice. I can deny my heritage—view it as a negative—and assimilate as best I can. Or I can take pride in who I am—part Jamaican and part African and part Puerto Rican… and part Scottish, believe it or not. And yes—I believe that 'retaining my strong sense of ethnic identity' is a very empowering response to the discrimination I face in America."

James didn't quite know how to respond and began a very awkward apology, which Martin quickly and mercifully put an end to.

"No—I'm sorry, James. I really appreciate all the help—you guys have all been great…," Martin said quietly as he looked away.

SCHOOLED!

"I just want you to pass this stupid test." James paused as he thought about what he wanted to say next. "Those kids... Martin... They really need..."

"Someone like me?" Martin asked with a faint smile.

James considered Martin's answer for a moment. "Yeah. They really do, Martin. Much more than they need someone like me."

Martin thought for a moment, took a deep breath, and smiled. "All right. I'll try to swallow my pride and choose *D* next time."

Later, as James watched Barbara Lemmons stumble through yet another rambling lesson, he felt genuine anger at the injustice of it all. How could the system employ this woman and even consider rejecting Martin King? How could anyone believe that a standardized test—particularly the LAST—had anything to do with teaching?

It didn't make any sense.

Robert was getting ready to take over the class, as it was his turn and the usual practice whenever Mrs. Lemmons became hopelessly lost, when something completely unexpected happened. A formally dressed gentleman holding a notepad came into the room, approaching Mrs. Lemmons with an outstretched hand and a smile that was a little too broad to be genuine. A look of wide-eyed terror came over Mrs. Lemmons's face as she shook the gentleman's hand and pretended as best she could to be happy to see him.

The man sat down in an empty chair near the front of the class, took out a pen, and began taking notes. James and Robert exchanged glances. This was a teacher observation. Mrs. Lemmons's class was going to be evaluated.

"This should be good," Robert whispered to James.

Mrs. Lemmons continued her incoherent lesson as before—only more loudly—and with a slight tone of desperation, James noted.

She injected as much energy into her lesson as was possible for an elderly woman—pacing back and forth and waiving her arms in the air, wide-eyed—speaking in heightened tones—but nothing she did changed the fact that she was incompetent. The lesson was incomprehensible—perhaps even more than usual as the added pressure of the situation was negatively affecting Mrs. Lemmons's limited ability to stay on track.

"Go see what he's writing down," Robert whispered.

James maneuvered himself to an area in the room where he could see what the evaluator was writing.

Robert would have done it himself, but it was James that had been gifted with better-than-average vision while Robert continually struggled with his thick prescription glasses—the victim of a family tradition of poor eyesight.

As the lesson mercifully drew to a close, James watched in utter disbelief as the evaluator checked off the box marked "satisfactory" on his evaluation sheet.

James was outraged.

Robert was more reflective. "I've heard that once you get tenure, they really don't mess with you because you basically can't get fired."

This made absolutely no sense to James, who came from a world where reasonably competent people were routinely fired for being only "reasonably competent."

The concept of tenure, James had always believed, was something that might have some importance in higher education as it allowed professors to publish controversial material without the fear of political reprisal. He failed to see how this concept applied to primary and secondary educators who never published anything and received tenured status almost automatically after just three years in the system or less in some states.

And if Mrs. Lemmons's evaluation was any indication, the selection process for tenure seemed ripe for political influence anyway. But more to the point, what was to stop a tenured teacher from slacking off or becoming abusive—or having some sort of mental breakdown as was the case with Mrs. Lemmons?

"Incompetent teaching isn't the worst offense you can commit as a tenured teacher—and you probably aren't going to get fired for it. They'll send you to a rubber room where you do nothing on full salary while waiting for a disciplinary hearing you'll almost always win." Robert studied the look of disgust on James's face. "Talk about a rigged court—I've heard the arbitrators that decide these cases are chosen by the local teachers unions and school districts—so they're pretty much beholden to them. I've even read about cases where teachers accused of sexual misconduct with students have kept their jobs."

James was confused and horrified. How did such a corrupt system evolve? How could people who were incompetent and even abusive be allowed to teach children?

Two weeks after Mrs. Lemmons passed her evaluation, Martin King faced the system as he took the LAST exam for his second and final chance to pass. A few weeks later, as the summer drew to a close, the cohort learned that Martin Monty King, the teaching fellows candidate with the most potential of them all, had failed the LAST again and would not be able to continue in the program. And there wasn't anything anyone could do about it.

The system had decided. Barbara Lemmons was in, and Mr. Martin Monty King was out.

As dispiriting as this was for everyone in the cohort and as unfair and irrational as it was to deprive Benjamin Harrison's students of Martin's many talents, it wasn't the worst thing the system would do to the still highly motivated group of teaching fellows that summer and to their hopes of making Benjamin Harrison a better school.

It was after the summer training had ended and James and Sue had gone to Montauk for a welcomed vacation that James got the call. Benjamin Harrison had decided not to hire James and the majority of the other teaching fellows for the fall.

As James understood the situation, under union rules it was an advantage for teachers to retire at the end of the summer so they could receive the maximum amount of retirement benefits. The policy left schools scrambling for replacement teachers at the beginning of the school year—and the teachers available at the last minute were mostly from "the bottom of the barrel"—people, as James's future mentor Leslie Brooks would explain to him, "You wouldn't want to hire to walk your dog."

So Benjamin Harrison took advantage of the Teaching Fellows program, promising the large, motivated group that positions would open up in the fall—but never did. The cohort scrambled to find teaching assignments for the fall and ended up scattered in schools throughout the city.

The team had been broken up.

Only Lauren Weiler and her faithful debate partner Gerald Houston remained at Benjamin Harrison. Robert found a job at another Bronx high school that James could never remember the name of. And James returned early to New York City from his much-needed vacation to undertake a job search before beginning one of the greatest challenges he would ever face.

CHAPTER 8

WELCOME TO EARL WARREN HIGH SCHOOL

There was a sort of cosmic irony that James would find a teaching position at Earl Warren High School. Although Earl Warren had the reputation of being one of the very worst high schools in the city, just behind Taft and Benjamin Harrison, the school wasn't located in a poor neighborhood.

Paradoxically, Earl Warren was located on the Upper West Side of Manhattan—home to many families and professionals who considered themselves upper middle class but who would probably be considered well-to-do in most other parts of the country. It was home to James's family, in fact, and smack in the middle of the neighborhood where James grew up and fairly close to where he now resided.

Earl Warren, however, served few people from the Upper West Side.

Its students came almost exclusively from poor neighborhoods in different boroughs throughout the city and were often required to make long subway commutes of well over an hour to attend.

James would occasionally wonder how the system could rationalize forcing students to travel such long distances to attend a failing school, but he was beginning to understand that many decisions the board of education made were simply not based on reason and that there was little point in trying to make any further sense of them.

James had always known of Earl Warren—vaguely aware of it during his childhood as an area of the neighborhood to stay away from—and as a place where one might see a fight after school. It was infamous to Upper West Siders who quietly bemoaned its existence within their gentrified neighborhood—especially when school was dismissed and throngs of teenagers would storm the uptown number one train, often causing delays with raucous and sometimes violent activity.

Physically, Earl Warren's complex contrasted greatly with the grand old building that was Benjamin Harrison. Although functionally very complete, including outdoor tennis courts that never seemed to be in use, Earl Warren was a concrete monstrosity built in the mid-1960s—its architectural design from the same institutional floor plan recycled from those of prisons and mental asylums, James imagined.

Indeed, Earl Warren did have the look and feel of a penitentiary with its slatted windows and heavily guarded metal detectors to greet its students at its front doors.

Any concerns James had about securing a teaching position at the last minute, with barely any previous teaching experience, proved to be unwarranted. James was hired immediately after a very brief interview with Earl Warren's principal, Dr. Rhonda White; a short, stocky, energetic woman in her early fifties who impressed James with her sharp mind and genuine commitment to turning Earl Warren around.

The school had recently, under her leadership, been taken off the city's infamous list of failing schools, and Dr. White was spearheading a plan to modernize the facility and generally improve the educational success of its students.

What struck James most about the hiring process was how eleventh hour it was. The start of the fall semester was just days away, yet the school still had many positions to fill—and for the opposite reason James and the others had been turned away at Benjamin Harrison—because many teachers had retired at the very last minute so they could get the maximum amount of retirement benefits—and a lot of vacancies at Earl Warren had suddenly materialized.

James would later tell Sue that just about anyone who was a certified teacher could have been hired when Dr. White went out of her way to comment how much better dressed James was than the other candidates she'd interviewed because James wasn't wearing a T-shirt, jeans, and sneakers—sporting, instead, slacks, an appropriate dress shirt, and a tie. James had actually dressed down from his three-thousand-dollar suit, sensing the attire was too formal for the teaching profession.

The experience left James wondering just what sort of people were applying for these last-minute teaching positions and how they had managed to get certified in the first place.

The rest of the hiring process moved very quickly, and James soon found himself sitting in his first meeting of the English department at Earl Warren High School.

James was happy to see some familiar faces from the Teaching Fellows program. Jan Walker, Jane Sherwin, and Andy Stein had originally been disappointed that they had been assigned to Earl Warren and had not been part of one of the larger teams of teaching fellows at Benjamin Harrison or Taft—but quickly realized they had lucked out once they began their student teaching.

"It's a school that's recently turned the corner, and we've gotten a lot of support here over the summer," Andy advised.

Andy Stein was a nonathletic version of Robert Sullivan: on the short side and a little more than slightly overweight as opposed to "wrestler stocky." Like Robert, Andy was quite nearsighted and wore thick glasses but, unlike James's wrestler friend, had a quiet demeanor and a subtle wit that was clever as opposed to attention seeking.

Jan Walker and Jane Sherwin generally agreed with Andy's assessment.

Jan Walker was one of the younger participants in the program, and James knew her only casually. She had graduated from Swarthmore and had been in publishing for a short time, deciding just a few months into her first job that the profession wasn't for her. She had decided to give teaching a try, motivated by her love of literature and by some positive experiences at a nonprofit tutoring center.

Jane Sherwin, conversely, had become one of James's closer friends in the program and had been the person who had excitedly called him about the opening at Earl Warren at the end of the summer. Jane had grown up in New York and had graduated from James's high school just two years behind James—and although the two had never socialized in those days, they were always vaguely aware of one another's existence, as Jane's older brother had been a member of James's graduating class. Jane had been in public relations for six years after graduating from UPenn but decided her career wasn't rewarding and was unlikely to become so—and that it was time for a major career change.

The four stood together as a group at one end of the cramped English department office, a space far too small for a meeting of the entire department and lacking nearly every creature comfort James was used to in an office, including a coffee machine, James lamented. Indeed, the majority of the space was dominated by old file cabinets and a small attached room full of dusty textbooks and piled-up boxes full of old Regents exams.

The rest of the faculty sauntered in one by one—greeted, sometimes with hugs and kisses—as they reunited after their long summer break. Gabrielle Williamson even showed up, mainly to say a tearful goodbye to all her former colleagues and to wish James—her replacement now that she had finally retired after thirty-one years—the best of luck.

Gabrielle was, by all accounts, a dedicated and talented teacher who would be sorely missed and whose shoes would be difficult for James to fill for more than just academic reasons. Gabrielle Williamson's retirement would leave Earl Warren—a school that served an almost entirely African American and Hispanic population—with just one African American teacher on its entire faculty, the rest of which was nearly all Caucasian.

Kevin Newcomb would lead his first faculty meeting that afternoon as the newly minted assistant principal (AP) of the English department. Kevin, James had learned, was replacing Mary Allen—known as just "Mary," her name spoken with an almost religious reverence by everyone— who had also retired that year and was much beloved by all.

Kevin had worked with Mary over the past year, learning the ins and outs of his new position, and had also elected to spend the summer at Earl Warren, making sure he and his department were ready for the fall term—so James was the only member of the faculty who Kevin hadn't officially met.

Jane Sherwin's take on Kevin was that he seemed dedicated and enthusiastic but also rather focused on advancing in his career and that she hadn't quite figured him out. Everyone agreed that he was organized and supportive—but this was his first foray into school administration, and James could sense a slight uneasiness among the faculty as Kevin went over his checklist of what remained to be done to prepare for the new term.

And beneath Kevin's slightly too confident facade, James could also sense that Kevin was feeling a little unsure of himself as the challenges and responsibilities of his new position were coming ever closer with the beginning of the new term looming just ahead.

Kevin was also relatively young—younger than many of the senior faculty he would be in charge of—although he could have easily been mistaken for a man well into middle age with his receding hairline and thick glasses that magnified the wrinkles around his eyes. Kevin had a good eight years of teaching experience under his belt, mostly in schools similar to Earl Warren and was known as being a good teacher, although his real desire was to be in school administration, with the career goal of being a high school principal someday.

He had grown up in Queens, had the nasally accent to match, and had done all his academic work at city and state colleges. Kevin seemed genuinely impressed with the academic credentials of his newest recruits, confessing to James that he had considered law school for a short time and had always wondered whether he had made a mistake not going, a sentiment he would repeat with ever greater frequency the further into the school year they progressed.

James and the other teaching fellows were assigned five classes of freshman English while the more senior faculty were assigned elective classes of juniors and seniors. The freshman classes were much harder to teach, but the easier assignments were, by tradition, given to more senior faculty, so the inexperienced teaching fellows would have to go through a trial by fire—and the kids who were most at need would get the least experienced faculty.

After the main meeting disbanded, Kevin kept James and the other teaching fellows for a private meeting of their own.

"This is just between us," he began. "I just wanted you to know that I couldn't be happier with the four of you coming to teach here. You're all obviously smart and talented and have a lot of potential. But there's a lot that can go wrong for a new teacher—especially in a place like this."

Kevin paused for a moment to take a long breath as he composed himself, then continued in a more pessimistic tone. "I want to stress that your teaching experience will be quite different during the regular school year than it was in the summer—and that there are things about the teaching profession and about the school system they probably didn't tell you in the Fellows program but that you need to know. It isn't politically correct to say this—but to survive in this system you need to understand that teaching has become a cover-your-ass profession."

Kevin let the phrase sink in for a moment.

James was reminded of Joseph Bile's frank talk about surviving the system—the honesty of which he appreciated but which also caused him apprehension about what was to come.

"Always document everything," Kevin continued. "It's sad, but the system is geared so that you, the teacher, will get blamed for everything that goes wrong in your classes whether or not it's your fault. So document everything. Keep copies of everything. If something happens in your class—a student threatens you or another student—write an incident report immediately and in as much detail as possible. Create a trail of evidence that's going to back up your side of the story."

Jane Sherwin exchanged slightly confused and worried glances with James.

Kevin went on. "Physical contact with students. I want to stress in the most serious way that you are never to touch a student—even in a customarily friendly way. If you do, you are taking a risk. If a teacher makes physical contact with a student and that student claims injury or molestation or whatever it is, it is the teacher that is going to get the blame, not the student—not the 'child'—again, regardless of fault, and regardless of what is fair and just, and regardless, by the way, if this 'child' is six foot seven, two-fifty, and has a lengthy juvenile record. Now, I'm not saying I would refuse to shake a student's hand if they offered it—but understand that you are taking a risk if you do."

Kevin directed his attention to James. "And James, you're a big guy, so I want to stress this especially to you—but to all of you just in case you get the idea that you want to be a hero and get in the middle of a fight. You will see fights break out at Earl Warren. And you may have the instinct to get in the middle of one to keep a student from getting hurt. And I'm telling you—just don't. One or all the students involved will claim that you hurt them when you inappropriately touched them, and they will sue the city and they will sue you. In addition to inviting possible criminal charges and the possible end of your teaching careers, should you get injured by getting in the middle of a fight, the injury will be considered your fault and you will find that getting compensation for such an injury will be nearly impossible. Again, you will be blamed regardless of how noble your intentions were. If you see a fight or witness students making physical threats, call security immediately. The security officers are members of the police department and have the authority to restrain students and make arrests if necessary. That is their job—not yours."

James, who had always strongly gravitated toward noncontact sports, such as his beloved swimming, had absolutely no intention of ever involving himself in a fight and risking physical injury—let alone legal liability. But Kevin's blunt talk did cause James to wonder about school safety—for both the staff and students—and he made a mental note to find out if anyone had ever been seriously injured at the school.

"And finally, grades. If you fail a student, don't make that decision lightly. Remember that you will be blamed for that failure—not the student. Not the 'child.' Whether or not that's fair is beside the point. It is your responsibility to make sure your students learn the material and pass your classes. If you do have to fail a student, be sure you can support that failure by maintaining a detailed grade book and attendance record. But understand that you can't just fail students because you don't think they meet what you would consider an appropriate standard—that is not your job. It is your job to get your students to the highest level possible and to advance them to the next grade. And make no mistake, we are judged by the percentage of students who pass and by the percentage who fail. To be clear, I'm not telling you how to grade your students—I can't do that. But understand that if you fail students, it will be seen as a reflection of you as a teacher—not of the student—not of the 'child' in your care. And if you have a high failure rate, you will have to justify that high failure rate to me."

Pressure not to fail students wasn't something that James had thought about before, and he was suddenly—and very uncomfortably—aware of the great conflict of interest that existed for both faculty and administration.

That evening, as James swam his four-thousand-yard workout in the century-old lap pool at the YMCA, he thought about the system and how it had so many incentives that worked the wrong way—especially the strong incentive to pass students along—irrespective of performance. But teachers and administrators needed to raise standards—not lower them—if they were going to improve the schools and best serve the interests of their students… Didn't they?

Sue's reaction was that Kevin was probably just "covering his own ass."

"Those kids are going to be very lucky to have you as a teacher. You're going to do great—and I'm really proud of you," Sue reassured him as she kissed him good night and went to bed.

But that night, James couldn't sleep.

The reality that he would soon be teaching five classes of freshman English and responsible for around one hundred and seventy students was beginning to weigh on him. What if this didn't work out? What if his young summer student Javier Ramos was right and he would have to become a strict disciplinarian in order to survive in a school like Earl Warren? Could he do that? Did he want to do that? He'd signed up to teach, not to yell at misbehaving kids for the rest of his working life. Maybe quitting law had been too rash a decision. Could he get back into the profession if he needed to? It might be impossible—and then where would he be?

Maybe this is just first-day jitters. It'll all work out somehow, James comforted himself as he closed his eyes and tried to sleep. But he wondered, as he went over in his mind his lesson plans for his first day of classes, whether the system Kevin had described that day would thwart even the best efforts of a dedicated faculty and administration to turn around a school like Earl Warren.

CHAPTER 9

DAY ONE—ROOM 237

James's first-period class—his first class as a new teacher—was in room 237—the irony of which was not lost on James. An avid Stanley Kubrick fan, James immediately recognized the room number—the same as the room number of the infamous haunted hotel room in Kubrick's horror movie, *The Shining*.

James was fairly certain that Earl Warren's room 237 wasn't haunted, but it wasn't a normal classroom either.

It was a double-sized room used by the drama club for rehearsals and performances—complete with a small stage area and a piano that was kept locked—thankfully!—during the regular school day. The room was meant to accommodate a much larger audience than the thirty-four ninth graders who now stared silently at James from their desk chairs, which occupied the front half of the enormous space.

It was obvious to James that room 237 was never meant to be used as a regular classroom as it contained no permanent blackboard—only a small temporary one on wheels that was insufficient for displaying much more information than James's last name and a homework assignment.

And as he wrote on that miniature chalkboard, trying to squeeze all the information for his first class onto that tiny piece of slate, he hoped that room 237—and to a larger degree his new, ever more daunting career—wouldn't turn out to be his own horror movie.

James's plan was to have everyone introduce themselves by answering a few basic questions he had listed on the remaining space on the temporary blackboard: their name, hobbies/interests, and their favorite book—and then work on the class contract for the remainder of the period.

But James had to get through attendance first.

Without Robert's assistance or a formal desk or lectern in room 237, attendance turned out to be much more unwieldy than James had expected it to be—and he wondered, briefly, how Mrs. Lemmons was getting along in her first-period class at Benjamin Harrison without his and Robert's help.

Although James was very fluent reading aloud and generally did a decent job pronouncing everyone's name, there were many names on the list with nonstandard spellings and some names that were unfamiliar to James—and James soon became painfully aware that his young students were taking glee in each stumble he made.

With attendance completed, James began the introductions. The honor of going first went to Roberta Gonzalez, whose tired eyes with their disinterested blank stare, combined with her makeup-slathered bad skin, made her look older than her fourteen years.

Indeed, as James looked around the room, he was struck by how worn out and unhealthy many of his students appeared to be. James couldn't help but wonder if this was the result of a poor diet, a stressful existence, or both.

Unfortunately, Roberta Gonzalez had added a little more anxiety to her already stressful life that morning by arriving late and had been forced to take the end seat in the front row near the door where James had decided to begin student introductions. Roberta rolled her eyes before reluctantly answering the questions James had written on the portable blackboard.

"Roberta Gonzalez. My hobbies and interests is shoppin', watchin' TV, and sleepin'. And I don't like no books, mister."

James had thought Roberta was joking at first and was a little sur-prised at the lack of a reaction from the other students but quickly realized that Roberta's answers were meant to be serious and had been taken as such by the class.

"Haven't you read anything in school that you've liked, even a little?" James tried.

Roberta's face contorted into an "I can't believe he just asked me that" expression. The class laughed.

"Okay— Well… Maybe we'll find something this semester that you'll enjoy reading."

"Books is wack, mister," Roberta contradicted, raising her hands in surrender and shaking her head.

James didn't quite know how to respond.

"She mean books is stupid, mister! Excuse my French!" Keisha Sanders blurted out across the room from the far end of the back row.

The class burst into laughter.

Keisha Sanders, a wiry, tall fourteen-year-old—intimidating on pur-pose in both dress and attitude—derisively stared James down from her back-row seat with a self-satisfied smirk. James, although inexperienced and with painfully little practical instruction in classroom management, understood he had to do something—and fast—or he was going to lose the class. Joseph Biles and Javier Ramos both flashed before his eyes. *Hit back*, he thought.

"I don't think you were actually speaking French—but you are excused this time, Ms.…"

James's comeback garnered scattered laughter of its own, and James knew that although he was on shaky ground, he was back in control for the moment. Keisha's smirk turned into a wide and very fake smile as she responded by introducing herself in a kind of a performance for the class.

"Hi, I'm Keisha Sanders, and I like clubbin', and I like shoppin', and I like singin' and dancin', and I don't have no favorite book 'cause books is mad wack!"

"Thank you, Keisha. But I would appreciate it if next time you wouldn't go out of turn," James responded, looking Keisha square in the eye.

Keisha was visibly a little surprised by James's quick, firm, yet polite response, and was about to return fire, but James was smart enough to avoid further confrontation and move on to the next student before she got the chance. Keisha, for her part, was content for the moment to rehash the incident in somewhat hushed tones with her good friend Tashecka Mills, who sat next to her in the back row.

Tashecka Mills contrasted with Keisha Sanders in both appearance and personality—much shorter than her tall, angular friend and some-what overweight—and unlike Keisha, not very verbal. Indeed, James often thought Kesha and Tashecka's friendship must have been based upon Keisha's constant need to talk—that Tashecka was her perfect silent part-ner as she was always there to listen but almost never had anything to say.

The two—Keisha doing most of the talking and Tashecka doing most of the giggling—would become a fixture in the back row of room 237 that would cause James much grief and consternation for the remainder of the term.

"Why don't we move on to this gentleman here?" James said as he pointed to the next student in the row.

Although James's instinct to keep the class moving was a good one, he had, unfortunately, called on Braxton Young—a sturdy fourteen-year-old whose features, including his large size and abundant, uneven facial hair, made him appear several years older. Braxton had also been late to class and, like Roberta Gonzalez, had been forced to take a seat in the front where he had immediately begun work on a sketch of a basketball sneaker. The act of drawing apparently consumed all Braxton's attention as James's presence in front of him failed to register even a small response. James tried again.

"So… Would you like to tell the class a little about yourself?" James asked, admiring Braxton's artwork as he waited for a response.

Braxton slowly looked up at James.

"Naa," was Braxton's monosyllabic answer as he went back to his drawing, garnering a few chuckles from the class.

"Okay… If you don't want to introduce yourself, could I at least get your name?"

Braxton didn't look up. He replied slowly, "Braxton. Braxton Young. I am present."

"That's a nice sketch, Braxton. Would you like to tell us about your interest in drawing?"

Braxton didn't look up.

"Braxton?"

James's persistence finally succeeded in getting a small amount of Braxton's consideration.

"I don't answer no questions, mister. Your questions is wack."

Braxton returned to his drawing. James took a deep breath; this wasn't working.

"Maybe I should introduce myself first," James suggested. Although the class barely reacted, James continued anyway. "My name is James Hartman. I'm participating in the New York City Teaching Fellows program, which recruits people from other fields to be public school teachers. Before I became a teacher, I worked as an attorney at…"

A confused babble suddenly rose from the class, as every student except for Braxton Young was suddenly paying attention. Keisha nearly fell out of her seat.

"You a lawyer, mister?" Keisha asked, wide-eyed and openmouthed.

"Yes. I'm a lawyer…"

"What happened? You got fired?"

The class roared with laughter, and even James had to smile.

"No, Keisha, I didn't get fired. I believe there are a few other attorneys in the Teaching Fellows program…"

"Well you should all go back to being lawyers, mister," Keisha instructed.

The rest of the class nodded in agreement. James didn't quite know how to react.

"The reason we decided to become teachers is that we all believe that public education is really important and…"

The entire class vocally expressed their disagreement.

"I wouldn't ever want to take care of someone else's kids," one girl called out.

"Yeah. It's hard enough me takin' care of my two little brothers when my mom's gotta work. I can't imagine babysitting a room full of strangers' kids," another concluded.

James's brow furrowed. "Wait. You all think the purpose of school is childcare?"

There was a general murmur of agreement—as if "childcare" was the obvious answer to the question: "What is the purpose of school?"

"You don't believe that education is the best path to achieving success? The American dream?" James asked, almost too bewildered to get the words out.

James was greeted with a louder murmur of disagreement and a few "boos."

"Not for us, mister. For you maybe," someone called out from the fourth row.

"Why not for you?" James countered.

"Look, mister— They put us here 'cause we ain't goin' nowhere in school. School ain't gonna give us nothin.'"

Although James had fully expected that many of his students would dislike school, the sentiments being expressed by his class went much further than that. This was a repudiation of the entire system. The majority of James's first class didn't believe in the very mechanism that society had set up to help them succeed in life.

And as James continued to listen to his students—whose comments were becoming increasingly animated—he realized this deep distrust extended to other parts of society as well—government, the police, the justice system… These were things designed, in the minds of many of his students, not to help but to oppress. And many of James's students, frighteningly, saw brighter futures in careers the street could offer them than the ones a college education could.

Others clung to dreams of playing professional sports or making it big in the music industry without having the slightest idea of what it took to make it in either of those highly competitive careers. The few students in the class who had college dreams were mostly pretty muted about them.

But it was a question that Keisha blurted out that really caught James off guard.

"If school so important, why all my teachers never go to college?"

Keisha's question was, perhaps, the most surprising to James, as he had assumed everyone knew that people in education *had* an education. Indeed, he assumed everyone knew that people who had careers almost always had an education—and was astonished to learn that many of his students didn't understand the connection between the two.

"They all went to college. In fact, they all went to graduate school after college. New York requires a master's degree to teach, so all your teachers either have an advanced degree or are in the process of getting one now."

Keisha was visibly shocked but recovered quickly. "Why they all stupid then?"

After the class finished laughing, there were some serious questions as to what an undergraduate degree was and what a master's degree was and what degrees James had as a lawyer. James was, again, surprised by the lack of basic knowledge students had about higher education.

Keisha wasn't impressed. "That a lot of school just to be a teacher, mister. I think you should go back to your law firm and beg for your old job back."

"In all seriousness, do you all realize how important it is to make sure everyone gets an education? That's why New York spends so much money on its public schools."

The class responded with a confused babble.

"They do?" someone called out.

"Yes. I believe New York spends close to twenty thousand dollars a year on each of you."

The confused babble got louder by a factor of three.

"They shouldn't do that, mister!" Keisha adamantly concluded.

"Yeah, just give me the money!" another student shouted out. There was overwhelming agreement from the class.

"Have you ever heard the expression 'give a man a fish, you feed him for a day. Teach a man to fish, you feed him for a lifetime?'" James tried.

"I still rather have the money!" someone called out.

"I don't want to be fishin'. I don't even like fish, yo!" another added.

The class seemed to be in unanimous agreement.

James, again, didn't quite know how to respond. It was going to take more than just a debate on the first day of class to convince his students that school was important. The class was getting out of control again, and James decided to change the subject.

"I'm sorry to hear that so many of you have had poor experiences in school. I hope this class can help change some of your minds about school and books. And to that end, I thought we would, together, come up with a class contract..."

The class booed.

"Why all our teachers make us do a class contract, mister?" a student called out.

"You just gonna do what you want anyway," another student added.

"I ain't signin' no contract without my lawyer!" Braxton Young announced in a huge, booming voice that filled the entire space of the double-sized classroom—all without looking up from his nearly finished drawing of a sweet-looking pair of Reebok Answer IV basketball sneakers.

Braxton's vocal projection would have been impressive even for a seasoned opera singer.

The word "contract" had succeeded in getting Braxton's attention— one of the few things James would ever say that would do so.

And with Braxton's sagacious legal advice and the cheers of support that followed, James knew he had lost the class. And he remembered what Joseph Biles had said to a skeptical audience of teaching fellows about losing a class on day one and never getting it back.

James was no longer a skeptic.

As the class continued to roar with laughter, the bell rang, signaling the merciful end to the period. And James—feeling physically beaten up and with a sensation of being close to tears he hadn't experienced since childhood—gathered his books and retreated back to the English department office.

CHAPTER 10

DAY ONE—THE REST OF THE DAY

If the rest of James's first day had been more of the same, he might have taken Keisha's advice and begged Phil Blake for his old job back. Fortunately for James, the rest of his first day as a teacher would bear little resemblance to his first-period class.

This was due in large part to Leslie Brooks, known to her students affectionately as "Mrs. Books," who greeted James as he retreated into the English department office. Her usual large coffee and bagel with cream cheese breakfast, purchased from the overpriced coffee shop across the street from the school, was spread out in a disorganized mess in front of her on one end of the lone table that sat at the far end of the small office.

James would, on most future mornings, playfully debate the value of Leslie's costly breakfasts and lunches she would always buy at the neighborhood restaurants that James knew she couldn't really afford—extolling the frugality of his own packed lunches. But Leslie would always insist that the cost of a nice breakfast and lunch was more than worth it for the amount of stress they would relive from the day—and the further along in the term James got, the more he understood Leslie's point.

Leslie was a woman of middle age who, despite her rapidly graying blond hair, still thought of herself as the twenty-something grad student she was back in the day, fighting the good fight to save the world from poverty and ignorance. Leslie was informal in the extreme, always slightly unkempt, and just a little too friendly and approachable for James's taste.

Although Leslie was generally laid-back and idealistic, she could occasionally be quite practical and almost uncomfortably conservative about education and the public school system—an outlook that Leslie admitted had changed over the years as she had gained more exposure to the realities of the system and the population schools like Earl Warren served.

Leslie's more practical side might have also been influenced by her good friend and colleague, Catherine Angel, who sat across from Leslie at breakfast, with only a small cup of hot tea in contrast to Leslie's expensive coffee and messy bagel and cream cheese.

Catherine's small stature and frail physique contrasted greatly with her taller friend's more comfortable figure, to the point that James wondered how such a tiny woman would ever be able to command the attention of a class like the one he had just experienced—that was until Catherine Angel commanded James's attention with her steely Southern accent.

"Get your ass kicked this mornin', Hartman?" Catherine inquired with a well-mannered smile as she sipped her tea.

Catherine Angel, known as "Ms. Angel my ass" to her students behind her back, had traditional and very formal Southern roots, which manifested themselves in both her dress and demeanor—both in and outside the classroom. And Catherine was quite conservative in her political views as well, which often resulted in friendly but spirited debates between Leslie and Catherine that both seemed to enjoy tremendously—which, combined with their shared professional interests, cemented a strong and enduring friendship.

"Don't rub it in, Cathy. Jim's a great guy, and he's gonna do just fine! Right Jim?" Leslie reassured as she toasted James with her Styrofoam coffee cup.

Leslie had taken an immediate liking to James—mainly because his name was "James," which meant she could call him "Jim," and "Jim" was short for Captain James T. Kirk of her beloved *Star Trek*—a show that Leslie, a devoted Trekkie, would constantly refer to in ways that often only fellow Trekkies could understand.

Indeed, Leslie would become genuinely baffled when ordinary people like James couldn't follow her train of thought every time she employed a metaphor that included an obscure reference to the show.

"So how'd it go, Jim? Mission accomplished or beam me up, Scotty?"

If there was one thing James disliked more than being called "Jim" it was *Star Trek*—a show that was hopelessly optimistic and just plain goofy. Still, he was appreciative of Leslie's genuine concern for his successful launch into the teaching profession—the beginning of his "mission to boldly go," as Leslie referred to it. And James was desperate for any help he could get.

James started explaining how things hadn't gone that well when Jane Sherwin, in tears, burst through the door, collapsing in a chair next to James.

"It's so different than in the summer! They were laughing at me! I tried doing the class contract…" Jane sobbed.

"I've never had any success with that," Leslie advised.

"Those kids are smart. They see a class contract as a gimmick—and they won't trust you to live up to it anyway."

Catherine Angel had a different take on class contracts. "There's no negotiation in my class. I tell my students what's required of them, and they either do the work or they fail my course. Simple as that."

Predictably, Leslie disagreed with Catherine's dictatorial teaching philosophy, and the two debated the issue briefly before arriving at the conclusion that James and Jane would ultimately have to find their own teaching styles.

This made sense to James. He wasn't by nature as strict as Catherine nor quite as informal as Leslie—but the class contract idea wasn't working for him and it needed to be ditched. Perhaps he could focus on introductions somehow.

Leslie offered a suggestion. "Instead of just calling on students, have them pair up and interview each other—like they were journalists for a newspaper. That way you've got them writing something down on paper while they're doing something fun. Just circle around the room to make sure everyone's on task."

Leslie's suggestion was rebuffed by Catherine, who disliked group work because it was too "messy" for her taste—and Leslie had to admit there was a risk of students becoming too social but that limiting the groups to two students would mitigate that problem, and the benefits would probably outweigh the costs.

Although James understood from the early days of the master's program that the formal education he was receiving was pretty worthless, it was becoming clear to him that using a university model to teach teachers might actually be detrimental, as it certified people as being qualified to teach who could negotiate all the academic hurdles but who had neither the hands-on experience nor the personality to be effective in the classroom.

And James wondered if such programs should be scrapped entirely and replaced by mentoring programs where prospective teachers could learn the realities of the profession—and discover whether they were really cut out to be teachers.

As James left the English department office on the way to his second class of his first day, he stopped for a moment to listen to Principal White's recitation of the Pledge of Allegiance echo through the halls of Earl Warren through its crackly PA system.

"I pledge allegiance to the flag of the United States of America…"

Not a single student took notice.

"One nation, under God…" Principal White continued in her signature monotone.

The Pledge of Allegiance and whether or not to include the phrase "under God" had been a major issue James had studied in law school, but the students at Earl Warren seemed completely oblivious to it.

And it didn't help that Principal White, although an intelligent and well-educated woman, had absolutely no oratory skills whatsoever—to the point that faculty meetings would often become a test of who could keep from nodding off if Principal White went on for too long.

What a waste, James thought as he considered the squandered effort and expense arguing over the constitutionality of the Pledge of Allegiance over many decades in various courts around the country.

As the Pledge of Allegiance crackled to a close and James arrived at his second class of the day, he was relieved to see that it would be held in a normal classroom with a real blackboard and a desk—and even more relieved to discover that all classes were not created equal.

Indeed, Leslie had suggested to a very skeptical James that he might have just gotten unlucky in his first class—that there was a sort of group dynamic where the balance of the class tipped toward interested students or against them—and that even a good, experienced teacher might have trouble when the balance of the class tilted the wrong way.

"It's awkward to say—but there are some kids that are just... bad. And I don't mean bad students—you'll get a lot of those and many of them are perfectly nice—some of my favorite kids, actually. What I mean is there are some kids that are just trouble. And some of them can pull a class down all by themselves. Conversely, if you have enough good students, they can help pull up the underachieving ones," was Leslie's assessment.

James thought of Keisha Sanders and Braxton Young. Both had the potential to wreck the class—and there didn't seem to be enough interested students in that group to shift the balance in the other direction.

To James's delight, the exact opposite was true in his midmorning class. Although there were some disinterested students who mostly sat quietly in the back, there were several students who would later make the honor roll and who were more than enthusiastic enough to motivate everyone.

Mark McAllen was one of the few Caucasian students at the school who would struggle socially but excel academically, mostly due to a good work ethic. And Mark had college aspirations, hoping to get a free ride somewhere because his parents couldn't really afford anything else—and use his math skills to become a CPA one day.

There was also Sophia Campbell, who had grown up in Jamaica and would end up making the Dean's list. Like Mark, Sophia also had college plans, but unlike Mark, Sophia was academically talented in addition to being hardworking.

But the real star of the class was Maria Rodriguez, a very petite girl with long black hair who could have been mistaken for a middle-schooler and whose lack of stature put her at a severe disadvantage in the overcrowded and often physically aggressive environment at Earl Warren.

Maria also had the unpopular distinction of being smart—very smart—having been an honors student throughout grade school and middle school and who couldn't help but participate in class, to the consternation of many of her peers.

Maria impressed James with her energy and enthusiasm but mostly with her raw intelligence—as Maria always seemed to have some new insight about whatever story or poem James would put in front of her. And unlike most of the smarter kids at Earl Warren, Maria was academically in excellent shape.

Maria also had college dreams. "My parents immigrated here when they were older and don't speak much English, so they never pursued a higher education. I want to be the first in my family to go to college. I want to make them proud," Maria declared with a beaming smile.

James was glad to have Maria as a student but also wondered how an academically talented kid like Maria could slip through the cracks and end up at a school like Earl Warren.

In addition to having many more interested students in his second class of the day, ditching the class contract also seemed to help, and Leslie's suggestion to pair students up for introductions went over well. Even James's own introduction went well—with a good discussion of what was required for college and law school, without any of the confrontation Keisha Sanders and company had provided in his first-period class.

Needless to say, James felt quite relieved.

The rest of the day also went well, but it was James's last-period class that had the most interesting group of students. The classroom was on the third floor, and as James bounded up the stairs, thankful for his regular swim workouts, he couldn't help notice that many of the teenagers he passed with surprising ease were struggling physically with the stairs—many wheezing and having to stop at each landing to catch their breath.

"Where the elevator at, mister?" was the usual query aimed at James as he sped by.

There weren't elevators available for the general population at Earl Warren—so unless a student could show they had a disability of some sort, they would have to get used to climbing the stairs.

James was again struck by how many of the kids at Earl Warren were in such poor shape, and when James eventually got to peek in on a physical education class, he saw part of the reason. The class was a disordered mess with students mostly just standing around for the whole period. As one student described their once-per-week gym class, "We spend most of the time just lining up."

The first student to greet James as he put his name on the blackboard and organized his desk for his last class of the day was Danielle Williams—dressed in too-tight jeans and a loosely fitting New York Knicks T-shirt, her broad smile gracing her friendly, round face as she noisily exaggerated being out of breath from her climb up the three flights of stairs.

An expression of confusion wrinkled her brow as she studied her new English teacher.

"Another White teacher? No offense, mister—but where are all the Black teachers at?"

"And you are…?" James began, trying to avoid the pointed question he didn't have an answer for.

"Danielle Williams. Why there ain't any Black teachers at this school, mister?" Danielle asked again sincerely.

"I'm not sure I have a good answer, Danielle. But "ain't" ain't really a word," James replied with a grin.

James hoped his correction would be taken in the lighthearted fashion in which it was given. And Danielle's faint smirk back told him that it had.

"Aren't. You're a new teacher, *aren't* you, mister."

"How can you tell?" James asked, a little defensively.

"Because you *AIN'T* yelled at me yet."

Danielle gave James a self-satisfied smile and took her seat in the front row.

Danielle's quick wit was genuinely amusing to James—but at the same time, he wondered how many teachers had actually yelled at Danielle, who seemed to James to be guilty of nothing more than having a good sense of humor and a strong personality.

Danielle always sat next to her childhood friend Gavin Mosley, a slender-faced kid whose friendly personality reminded James of Javier Ramos at Benjamin Harrison, only without the obsession with the New York Yankees. Danielle and Gavin paired up and interviewed each other for introductions. Gavin went first.

"My partner is Danielle Williams. She likes shopping and dancing—is a pretty good singer—and is a big New York Knicks fan as you can tell by her shirt. And Danielle wants to go to college and become a doctor someday."

"It's a lot of years in school and a lot of hard work, but if you really want to be a doctor, you can if you put in the effort," James commented.

Danielle grinned. "I will be a doctor someday, and nothin's gonna stop me!"

The class applauded as Danielle turned to introduce Gavin.

"My partner and good friend is Gavin Mosley, and he also likes the Knicks—or I'd kick his you know what—and his favorite food is pizza, and his favorite place is Great Adventure, and he don't know what he wants to be when he grows up."

"But I know I want to go to college someday," Gavin added.

James was both happy and relieved to hear several of his new students express an interest in college. And the enthusiastic responses of many of the other students also pointed to a successful last-period class—except for one quiet student who sat in the back row, introduced unenthusiastically as Jimmy Wiggins.

"This is Jimmy Wiggins. And he don't have much to say about himself."

James studied Jimmy Wiggins, a somewhat heavyset young man dressed in worn, mismatched clothes that looked as if they had been recycled through the Salvation Army more than once. A faint smile graced his round face, but it was betrayed by his melancholy eyes, which looked tired and hopeless and on the verge of giving up in the great race of life at the tender age of fourteen.

James sensed there was something wrong and decided to press further. "How about a favorite thing you like to do?" James suggested.

Jimmy just shrugged.

"A lot of students like going to Great Adventure. Do you like amusement parks, Jimmy?"

"I'm sorry, mister. Ain't never been to no amusement park. Don't really do much."

"How about your favorite food. Everyone's got a food they really like."

Jimmy shrugged. "Don't really matter none, mister. Chocolate cake, I guess."

James decided that "chocolate cake" was about all the information he was going to get out of Jimmy Wiggins that first day but made a note to himself to find out more about the quiet kid with the sad face who sat in the back of his last-period class.

The rest of the class went well, although it was a little noisier than all but his first class, which was to be expected as it was at the end of the day, James rationalized to himself. The only odd thing was at the end of the class, James discovered that an energy bar he had brought with him for an afternoon snack had mysteriously disappeared from his desk.

"You lose somethin', mister?" Danielle asked on her way out.

"Nothing important. I had an energy bar... I know I put it down right here..."

"You think somebody took it?"

"An energy bar...?"

"Could be somebody took it. A lot of us get lunch at ten thirty, but nobody's hungry for lunch in the morning, so everyone's mad hungry by the end of the day 'cause we ain't... *haven't*... eaten nothin' since breakfast," Danielle corrected herself with a smile.

"Haven't eaten anything. Otherwise it's a double negative," James responded as he packed his books up for the day.

Danielle paused for a moment to review what she had just said—and grinned. "You mad funny, mister. See you tomorrow."

As James gathered his things, he congratulated himself on a mostly successful first day but wondered about the school's lunch policy.

If the kids were hungry enough that someone would take his energy bar—something they would be rather disappointed with once they bit into it, James imagined—perhaps he should give them a small snack before class. James knew that Principal White had a policy against food in the classrooms, but if his students were hungry, they weren't going to learn anything. So James made a note to himself to think of some discreet snacks he could offer to his last-period class as a way to both solve the hunger problem and build trust with his students.

After school, James found himself with the other teaching fellows, Leslie Brooks, Catherine Angel, and Norman Griffon, another long-time English teacher at Earl Warren at the Starving Writer, one of several trendy bars near the school that did a substantial business serving Earl Warren's stressed-out faculty and administration.

Indeed, James would continually be surprised by how much his new colleagues drank—and sometimes smoked, littering the back entrance of the school with their cigarette butts—due to the many pressures they faced on the job.

"Don't worry too much. He's just covering his own ass!" was Leslie's assessment of Kevin's dire portrayal of the teaching profession over drinks she insisted on buying for James and the other three teaching fellows.

The Starving Writer was Leslie's favorite watering hole near the school, partially because it was in an architecturally interesting turn-of-the-century building made to look like an old English pub but mostly because the specialty drinks were named after famous authors.

James nursed his Robert Frost, a vanilla vodka, multi-liquor and fruit juice concoction that James would probably not have enjoyed even if it had been later in the day and possibly even if he had been a drinker. He looked over at Jane, who was happily taking very generous sips of her Emily Dickinson, and Andy, who he could tell was feeling the effects of his fittingly potent Edgar Allen Poe. Jan also seemed to be enjoying her Emily Brontë, and Leslie was already on her second Jack Kerouac. Catherine had opted for Tennessee whiskey on the rocks, which she dubbed a "Tennessee Williams," while Norman sipped a club soda as usual because he was a recovering alcoholic, one addiction of many he had picked up in his youth while touring with a moderately successful rock band in the early '70s.

"So everything Kevin said isn't really true?" Jane asked Leslie hopefully.

"No—it's all true. He's right about everything he said. And I'd take his advice—especially as a first-year teacher. But you can't get all paranoid either. You're here to teach—not to just play it safe and 'cover your ass.' Drink up, Jim!" Leslie commanded, pointing to James's nearly full glass of the Robert Frost concoction.

James took a polite sip.

"You're not really a drinker are you, James. Don't worry. A year or two at Earl Warren and you'll be knocking them back just fine and dandy," Leslie exclaimed as she took another generous sip of her own drink.

Jane downed the rest of her Emily Dickinson. "I'm knocking them back already! I can't believe how different today was than teaching in the summer!"

Leslie signaled for another round for Jane. "Always remember—now that you've all begun your 'mission to boldly go'—it's not about changing the world or the system or even Earl Warren, it's about helping a few kids make a better life for themselves. If you can say you've helped improve the lives of just a few students at the end of your long trek through this profession, you can say you've had a successful career as a teacher. And if you can't accept that reality, you'll burn out after three years—just like the original series."

James reflected on Leslie's advice—an oft-repeated mantra that James would also hear from other successful teachers, minus the *Star Trek* references. And he thought about the many differences between his summer experiences and his first day as a new teacher at Earl Warren. "The classes were different—and most of the summer school teachers seemed different too... At least at Benjamin Harrison—they were mostly pretty bad. That doesn't seem to be the case here," James stated pensively as he nursed his drink.

"Speaking for myself, I'd have to be pretty desperate for money to teach in the summer. Most teachers just want to run away by the time summer rolls around. It's one of the great perks of the profession. You'll see," Leslie replied, offering her glass as a toast before downing the rest of her drink and signaling for another.

Catherine took a sip of her whiskey and added, "It's mostly the bottom of the barrel that sticks around for summer work. There are a lot of—we'll call them 'sketchy'—people in the system who managed to get certified somehow, and when there's a short supply of teachers, like in the summer or at the beginning of the school year, they get hired because there isn't any other choice. By the way, did anyone ever tell you guys to look out for squinting?"

The blank stares from James, Jane, Andy, and Jan told her nobody had.

"If you see kids squinting—especially from the back row—it means they can't see the board. A lot of our kids would rather be legally blind then wear glasses in front of their friends. Some may not have any to wear. So if you see squinting kids, move them to the front."

"What about thumb sucking?" Jane asked. "I noticed a lot of my kids doing it—it seemed really strange to me."

Leslie and Catherine exchanged glances. Leslie replied, "It could mean abuse of some sort. It isn't definitive though—it isn't something you'd report like bruising. But you might want to keep an eye on them."

James had noticed a few of his students with this peculiar habit, including Keisha Sanders and Braxton Young, and had dismissed it as unimportant at the time. But Jimmy Wiggins had also been one of those students—falling asleep toward the end of class with his head on his desk and his thumb in his mouth. Leslie's best advice was that James's instincts were probably good and that he should keep an eye on Jimmy and try to contact his parents.

Later that evening as James swam his four-thousand-yard work-out at the YMCA, he wondered what Jimmy's story was. Was he abused? Neglected? Homeless? He was determined to find out.

Sue's concerned reaction was that James should definitely call Jimmy's parents. And later that evening, James did call Jimmy Wiggins's home.

James didn't quite know what he was going to say to whomever picked up, but something inside him thought it important to make contact with Jimmy's caretakers anyway. As it turned out, the phone just rang and rang during the three attempts James made that evening—the same that would happen every other time James would telephone Jimmy's home.

The mystery of Jimmy Wiggins, James feared, was far too deep and complicated to be solved with a simple telephone call.

CHAPTER 11

THE GIFT OF THE MAGI

The next several weeks were challenging for James but mostly successful—except for his first-period class, which despite James's best efforts, continued to spiral downward into anarchy. Keisha Sanders and Tashecka Mills didn't even pretend to whisper anymore, especially, it seemed, when talking about the intimate details of their ostensibly very prolific sex lives, which James did his very best to ignore whenever possible.

Braxton Young mostly stayed quiet so long as he was left alone to listen quietly to his Discman and sketch sneakers. Few of his other students had any interest in even pretending to pay attention, and James found himself continually putting out small brushfires of disruption and teaching very little English.

The large empty space in the back of room 237 proved to be so much of a distraction that several students decided one morning to play a game of tag in lieu of English class, necessitating the assistance of two security guards who had to give chase in the tradition of the Keystone Cops, instigating raucous laughter from everyone except the busily sneaker-sketching Braxton Young before finally rounding up the easily winded students and escorting the wheezing, giggling lot of them to the Dean's office.

James was beginning to worry that if things didn't settle down in room 237, he might actually get fired.

James thought of the advice Javier Ramos and Joseph Biles had given him that summer about the realities of classroom management and how he had been so quick to dismiss that advice.

How clueless he had been!

As an outsider, he had been quick to blame student misbehavior on bad teachers. The reality of how commonplace serious behavioral issues were at Earl Warren had been shocking to James and the other new teachers at the school—and sometimes frightening.

Fights occurred often and could happen without warning. Disrespectful behavior toward teachers, administrators, and other students was the norm, with students often becoming astonishingly hostile for little or no reason.

To James, it felt as if the whole place were teetering on the edge and ready to explode.

James's first serious incident—a vicious fight that resulted in students being taken away in handcuffs—predictably involved Keisha Sanders and another girl who wasn't part of James's class but who had made the unfortunate decision to follow Keisha into room 237 one morning to continue their quickly escalating argument over some senior they both claimed as their boyfriend, whom James would later observe amorously kissing a third party.

James tried to play diplomat and calm things down between the two girls but was completely ignored and frantically called for security as Keisha and her nemesis went at each other with an energy and viciousness that left spattered blood and large tufts of hair on the floor.

Some teachers dealt with behavioral issues by employing dictatorial classroom management techniques à la Joseph Biles that would shock an outsider—which most of the time produced orderly classes but also resulted in far less instruction taking place as learning took a back seat to order.

Teachers with less disciplinarian personalities like James struggled daily with classroom behavior—using the few tools they had to deal with disruptive students such as rearranging seats, making compromises, and telephoning parents when things got really bad.

But truthfully, the teachers at Earl Warren had astonishingly little power to deal with students who acted out—and everyone—even good, experienced teachers—faced challenges from disruptive students in their classes on a daily basis which they sometimes could not control.

It was obvious to James that part of the problem was overcrowding.

James and the other teaching fellows, even without much in the way of classroom management training, hadn't experienced any serious behavioral issues over the summer because their classes were small and they could give students the individual attention they needed to focus on the work.

The other part of the problem—the touchier and politically very sensitive part of the problem—was about 10 percent of the student population who seemed to come to school only to cause trouble and to avoid truancy violations.

Although this wasn't correct to say or even think, James was beginning to understand that many of his assumptions about the public school system and about education in general were often factually incorrect. He understood what many veteran teachers already knew but could never say publically—that there were some students who were never going to be helped, who didn't want help, and who were going to put the education of the other 90 percent of the student population at risk, often on purpose.

And James lamented that public schools, unlike charter schools or private schools, couldn't manage their student populations—or their teacher populations—to weed out the 10 percent or so of each that endangered the education of everyone else who wanted to succeed.

One of the most frustrating setbacks for James, however, came not from a member of his out-of-control, first-period class but from a member of the administration, one of the 10 percent who would have been weeded out long ago in another environment. It happened, ironically, on a morning James had finally gotten everyone in room 237 to calm down somewhat and even display a small amount of interest in his lesson covering a poem by Langston Hughes.

As James was discussing the meaning of the last line in Hughes's poem "Harlem (Dream Deferred)," which asks if a dream deferred will "explode," the door to room 237 exploded open and Dean Richard Emerson burst into the room, screaming a tirade of rules and regulations at the top of his lungs, repeating the word "hats" over and over again—all directed, as if out of James's worst nightmare, at Braxton Young.

Braxton had, indeed, been wearing his hat in class over the past several weeks. And James, aware of the school policy against the wearing of hats, had, indeed, politely asked him to remove it the first time Braxton had donned it in class only to be met with an angry stare from Braxton who loudly—to the delight of everyone—declared that James was "wack" and continued on with his drawing as if nothing had happened.

At the time, James had decided to let it go—concluding that a battle with Braxton Young over his hat was a battle he couldn't win. And so long as Braxton wasn't disrupting the class, he was content to allow him to break a rule or two. Unfortunately for James, Dean Richard Emerson didn't share his classroom management philosophy.

Dean Richard Emerson, who insisted on being called "Dick," a name which perfectly suited him, was one of the few people who worked at Earl Warren who James felt shouldn't be working in education—or anyplace else that required brains, responsibility, or maturity.

Dick was aging poorly. He was a short, overweight, rapidly balding man of middle age and would continually attempt to resolve his seemingly profound middle-age crisis by taking his frustrations out on whatever students or faculty he could find that weren't in compliance with even the most insignificant rules and regulations.

And the wearing of hats in school was, apparently, at the top of Dean Dick's list of serious violations.

Before James even knew what was happening, the squat little Dean had bounded across the room at surprising speed to the back row where Braxton Young was quietly drawing as usual. Dick's mostly bald, over-sized head, reddened from all the yelling and screaming, was suddenly in Braxton's face—a decidedly unwise move in James's estimation. But the situation was well out of James's control, and he stood by and watched as the carnage ensued.

Braxton did not take the confrontation well, staring Dick Emerson down and telling him several times to "Back the fuck off, motherfucker!" before Dick Emerson finally did and called security to escort Braxton to the Dean's office.

But the incident didn't end there.

"Mr.… what's your name? Hartman! In the hallway—now!"

Although James did not appreciate being treated like a child in front of his class—or in general, for that matter, and internally had the very same reaction to Dick Emerson as Braxton—he nevertheless dutifully followed his Dean to the hallway as instructed.

"Ooooh! Mr. Hartman in trou-ble!" Keisha Sanders squealed with delight as she watched James exit the classroom.

James had expected Dean Emerson to calm down so they could have a professional discussion concerning Braxton Young and classroom management. But Dick Emerson was having none of it and proceeded, like a bad parent, to berate James for not being strict enough about enforcing the rules of the school. There was no discussing the matter.

"And when you don't enforce the rules—you make my job harder! You understand, Hartman?" Dean Emerson admonished, wagging his index finger at James.

James understood all too well that his problem class was going to be an even bigger problem now that Dean Dick had enforced his petty rule on hats—and that any modicum of respect James had from that group of kids was gone forever.

Fortunately for James, his other classes were going quite well, although James was surprised at how much work he was putting into them. Original, creative lesson plans had to be made every day, and James realized English wasn't the easiest subject to teach as there were an infinite number of ways to approach writing and literature. It wasn't like math or history where a teacher could rely on a textbook at least most of the time.

"You ever coming to bed, honey?" was Sue's usual signal to James that he'd gone past midnight, struggling to compose lesson plans for the following day.

Even with all the effort, James was often surprised at what worked and what didn't in the reality of the classroom. Leslie promised that after a few years it would get somewhat easier—mainly because James would have a lot of material he could draw upon for future classes and have a better sense of what techniques would be most effective given his particular circumstance.

Additionally, James found correcting assignments to be enormously time consuming—especially essays because they were nearly always riddled with mistakes and to be painstakingly corrected line by line—even papers written by many of his better students. And James was shocked by the content of the first student papers he corrected—a short in-class assignment where he had asked students to write creatively about their lives.

James had designed his first assignment as a way to get to know his students better. What James found in paper after paper was that the story of his students' lives was a story of violence and danger—a story of broken neighborhoods where street gangs fought over territory and drive-by shootings were commonplace.

Maria Rodriguez's grammatically flawless paper—the only one in all his classes that didn't require corrections—caught James's attention in particular.

When thinking about my life, I was reminded of the poem by Robert Frost you showed us in class called "The Road Not Taken" where a traveler comes to a place in a yellow wood where two roads diverge and is forced to make a choice: take the commonly traveled path or "the one less traveled by." We talked in class about the paths as a metaphor for choices we must make in life and empathized with the speaker's quandary.

But I was silently envious of the speaker.

My life isn't a yellow wood with idyllic trails that lead to a destination. It is a jungle where the underbrush is thick and where there are no roads to show you the way out. It is a dangerous jungle, filled with poverty, desperation, and violence. And it is a forgotten jungle, even though it is part of a shining city of opulence and splendor.

I wish my life were a walk in the woods and my greatest predicament choosing whether to be a lawyer or a poet. I wish I were bigger and stronger so that I could have a better chance of surviving in this wilderness. And, most of all, I wish there were roads to follow so that I could, one day, get out of this horrible place.

As revealing and emotionally moving as Maria's paper was, it was an essay James assigned using the story "Gift of the Magi" in his last-period class that would prove to be the most eye-opening.

James had garnered a lot of good will from his last-period class with his solution to their hunger problem. He had invested in a bulk purchase of small bags of pretzels, chips, and other nonsugary snacks designed to get his kids through their last class of the day and made his class promise to be discreet while eating them and not to make a mess—a promise they dutifully kept in exchange for the free food.

The only odd thing was that his own healthier snacks would still sometimes disappear by the end of the period. James couldn't imagine that his kids would like his health bars or baggies of nuts and raisins—but if they were keeping a child from going hungry, he wasn't going to complain.

James had chosen "Gift of the Magi" as the inspiration for the first take-home essay; the famous story about a poor young couple who each must sell their most valuable possession in order to buy the other a gift for Christmas. Ironically, each of their gifts is connected to the other's most valuable possession they've now sold, so the gifts themselves become worthless—but the love they demonstrate for one another turns out to be the best and most priceless gift of all.

The class loved the story, although James was surprised that no one had heard it before. James began the discussion by asking the class if they had ever received a gift that meant a lot to them. Gavin Mosely told the story of how he really wanted a fancy robot he had seen in a store for Christmas but knew it was too expensive for his mother to afford, as she was just a single mom. But that Christmas, Gavin unwrapped his present and the robot was inside.

Ironically, it didn't work very well and his mother ended up returning it—but Gavin got the gift of knowing how much his mother loved him because she had sacrificed so much to get him such an expensive gift.

"And that was much better than the robot," Gavin said with pride, to the applause of the class.

Danielle Williams told the story of how her mother had always tried to give her the gift of an education by reading to her every night and helping her with her homework the best she could. Her mother, also a single mom, had been a high school dropout, and now that Danielle was in high school, the work was becoming too difficult for her mother to help her with.

"She really wants to give me the gift of a college education. Ain't nobody in my family never... There *hasn't* been anybody in my family who *ever* went to college." Danielle proudly corrected herself.

"Well, if you ever need any extra help, Danielle, just ask. I think most of your teachers would be happy to give any of you extra help if you need it," James replied, nodding earnestly.

James had the class write their gift stories as a homework assignment to be started during class. It was a relatively fun and not particularly difficult writing assignment, and most of the class needed little coaxing to begin their essays.

Jimmy Wiggins was the exception. A sad look of hopelessness graced his round face as he looked down at his blank sheet of paper. James went over to help.

"Nobody ever give me no gift, mister. Ain't got nothin' to write about."

"It doesn't have to be recently. When you were a kid maybe?"

Jimmy shrugged his shoulders, his faint smile betrayed by his despondent gaze down at his empty page. And his reply struck James as being very matter-of-fact. There was no anger or sadness in his voice— Jimmy Wiggins was just stating the happenings of his life the way they were. Nothing more, nothing less.

"Ain't nobody ever give me no gift. Never celebrated no Christmas. Never celebrated no holidays—nothin'. Ain't got nothin' to write about, mister."

It was slowly beginning to dawn upon James that Jimmy's situation was more than just sad—it was dire. He tried again.

"What about a birthday party. You could write about a favorite birthday you had as a child."

Jimmy's expression remained fixed, and he again answered in the same dispassionate tone—replying to his visibly shocked teacher honestly, relaying the information in the same way he might have told James the day of the week or the month of the year.

"Ain't never had no birthday party, mister. Ain't got nothin' to write about."

For someone who had been brought up in James's world—or any world that had loving parents in it—the idea of a child growing up without ever having a birthday party was almost inconceivable. And James understood that Jimmy Wiggins, at the tender age of fourteen, was alone in the world—and probably had been for some time, perhaps his entire life.

James suggested that Jimmy write about a special gift he would like to give to someone someday as he had never received a gift of his own. James's suggestion seemed to go over well, and Jimmy began to write.

James, with emotions ranging from frustration and anger to sadness and resolve, decided to make it his business to find Jimmy Wiggins's date of birth—which, to his relief, was in just a couple of weeks on a Friday, so James could throw Jimmy a little birthday party at the end of class. It was a small gift he could give to Jimmy Wiggins. He wished he could do more—but he was determined to do something.

But a birthday party for Jimmy Wiggins wouldn't be such a small gift after all—not to Jimmy Wiggins—as James would first discover when he read Jimmy's finished paper. The first line printed in poorly handwritten pencil read:

IF I WAS TO GIVE A GIFT TO SOM ONE, I WOOD GIVE A BIRFDAY PARTY TO SOM ONE LIKE ME.

CHAPTER 12

THE THREAT

After Dean Dick's public scolding of Braxton and James, it was no surprise that James's first-period class deteriorated even further, almost to the point of being unteachable. It was, truthfully, near chaos, with students doing pretty much whatever they wanted and with almost no instruction taking place.

Every morning, James dreaded the prospect of either Principal White or Kevin coming around to observe the bedlam—and losing his job the following day.

James had taken the time to observe Leslie and Catherine's classes in search of some magic bullet that he was missing from his cobbled-together arsenal of classroom management techniques—but to his dismay, he couldn't find any. Indeed, the only thing James learned from watching the two veteran teachers was that there really wasn't any one teaching style that worked.

Leslie had a very loosely structured class that was a little noisy and chaotic for James's taste—but her kids loved her and the work they produced was of surprisingly high quality. Catherine was the polar opposite, sitting at her desk old-school and so strict that James was even a little intimidated. But her students also produced very high quality work, one of whom commented to James that Catherine Angel was "mad strict, but you learn a lot."

James had tried everything he could think of in his morning class, including switching students' assigned seats and telephone calls to parents—but nothing he did proved to be more than just a temporary fix. His efforts were sometimes even counterproductive and, in one case, disturbing.

Keisha Sanders and Tashecka Mills had been even louder and more obnoxious than usual when James requested that they sit apart one Wednesday morning. Predictably, they refused. Or more accurately, Keisha refused.

"Why you care, mister? Nobody here care about your stupid class!"

Tashecka concurred with a loud giggle.

"Look, Keisha. I've tried to be polite, but I can't have you disrupting the class…"

"Ain't no 'class' here, mister. You ain't doin' nothin'. You think you all that 'cause you got this job and shit? Fuck you!" Keisha shouted while giving James the finger.

Tashecka concurred with a louder giggle.

James called security and had Keisha removed for the day.

Later that evening, James called Keisha's parents.

James had attempted to contact Keisha's parents before but had been unsuccessful—once getting Keisha herself on the phone, to Keisha's great amusement. But this time a woman answered in a tired, irritated voice.

"What?"

"Hello, is this Mrs. Sanders? Keisha's mother?"

"Yeah. What she do now?"

James began to explain what had happened, but it became immediately clear that Keisha's mother was no longer paying attention to James as she had put down the telephone receiver to go search for her daughter. And James could only listen as the scene unfolded—and get an uncomfortable glimpse at what life was like in Keisha's world.

"Keisha! Where you at! Keisha!"

"What?"

"That another teacher on the phone! What I told you? What I told you?"

"It wasn't like that, Mama…"

"Shut up! I told you I don't want no more phone calls from no more teachers! You hear me?"

James was powerless to do anything as the two yelled back and forth at each other for the next couple of minutes. There was a lot of screaming and crying—and it sounded to James as if Keisha's mother had thrown something and possibly hit her daughter toward the end, although he had no way of knowing for sure. Eventually someone hung up the telephone, and James was left feeling horrible and with absolutely no clue about what to do about Keisha Sanders.

The next day, Keisha was completely silent and just glared at James.

James looked for any signs that Keisha had been physically abused during the fight with her mother, which he would have been required to report, but didn't see anything. Keisha's mother's discipline would last exactly one day, after which Keisha was worse than ever.

Leslie Brooks, after listening to James's latest horror story out of room 237, prescribed an after-school drink at the Starving Writer.

"I don't know if Kevin would fire you… Maybe he would. His ass is on the line if you screw up in front of Dr. White. Then again, you're doing well in your other classes and you have the potential to be a really good teacher," Leslie reflected as she patted James on the shoulder.

James took a polite sip of the beer Leslie had insisted on buying for him.

"Not even beer? You really aren't a drinker, Jim. I give you a year."

"I just don't know what else I can do, Leslie. I mean, I finally got through to Keisha's mother and…"

"Yeah. Sometimes that can backfire. It sounds like a nightmare of a class. Still, there are some strategies… Tell you what. Why don't I take the conn one morning later this week? *Stardate: Armageddon!*" Leslie suggested in an eerily spot-on William Shatner impression.

"Come again?"

"I'll guest teach your class. That way I can get a sense of what the problems are and help you get the old starship back on course. Maybe."

"You'd really do that?"

"Sure. I'd love to, Jim."

Leslie's guest teaching appearance was an interesting one for James to watch. While Leslie employed several familiar strategies for restoring order, including reassigning the seats of several students and demonstrating the capacity to be a lot stricter than James ever thought she was capable of, Leslie, even with her many years of teaching experience, could not completely control Keisha, Braxton, and company—especially when she dared separate Keisha and Tashecka for talking too loudly, moving Keisha to the front row—something Keisha seemed to take personally.

"Who you think you are, bitch?"

Keisha was removed for the day, and Leslie had to resort to handing out work sheets midway through the class instead of having the group discussion she had originally planned.

"It's a terrible space, and you have a lot of problem kids in that class," Leslie concluded, shaking her head in frustration.

"That girl Keisha's trouble—and I'm not quite sure what's going on with that kid Braxton—your artist in the back row. You'll never completely get them back to having a normal class—so I'd suggest work-sheeting them."

By "work-sheeting," Leslie meant having highly structured classes involving mini lessons and work sheets to be completed and handed in every day. Although not an ideal solution, the work sheets would keep the class occupied enough so that the kids would settle down and some instruction could take place. The work-sheeting solution would also cost

James more than a small amount of money in photocopying, as he would quickly run through his meager budget for copies at the school.

Indeed, James was beginning to discover that in addition to being underpaid, public school teachers were often expected to supplement deficiencies in classroom supplies with their own money—something Sue seemed to understand and complain about at the same time.

"I don't know how public school teachers afford to live in this city," Sue would often remark while paying the bills and noting the ever-increasing charges for stationary and art supplies on the American Express.

Fortunately, the added expense of Leslie's work-sheeting strategy turned out to be worth it for James, and over the next couple of days the class calmed down to the point where some instruction was actually taking place. As Leslie predicted, it wasn't an ideal situation. But it was an improvement James was quite happy with—until Braxton Young decided to make things a lot more difficult for him one Monday morning.

After Dean Dick Emerson's tirade, Braxton had been forced to do away with his hat, but his behavior was otherwise unchanged. He continued to have no interest in participating in class despite James's daily efforts to coax him into doing schoolwork and several unsuccessful attempts at getting ahold of Braxton's parents who never seemed to be home.

That horrible Monday morning, class began as it normally did for Braxton. He sat in his usual seat at the far end of the back row, sketching sneakers and quietly listening to music through his headphones.

Listening to music in class was, like the wearing of hats, against school policy. And if Dick Emerson had ever caught Braxton doing it, he would have popped a vessel, James mused. But James had dutifully attempted to separate Braxton from his Discman some time ago as he had tried to separate him from his hat only to be rebuffed loudly in front of the class and not listened to.

And again, James felt as if this were a battle he couldn't win and was content to let Braxton break a few rules in the interest of keeping the peace, despite what Dean Emerson might have to say.

Unfortunately, Braxton Young would not be content with James's compromise. Perhaps it was revenge for Dean Emerson's obnoxious enforcement of the rule on hats, or perhaps it was just because Braxton enjoyed the attention he garnered from disrupting classes. But Braxton decided that Monday morning to start James's week off on a really horrible note.

Braxton sat down and began sketching as usual, and James had attempted to get him to pay attention to the lesson, also as usual. And as usual, Braxton told James he was "wack" and continued sketching his latest rendering of a Nike basketball sneaker. And class would have gone on normally, except that for whatever reason, Braxton decided to misbehave just enough that James would have to confront him about it.

Braxton decided that soft music wasn't good enough for him that Monday morning and turned his Discman to full volume which, even though Braxton was wearing headphones, was loud enough for the entire class to clearly hear. A few students even started singing along to the music. James approached Braxton.

"Excuse me, Braxton?"

Braxton didn't respond.

"Hey, Braxton," James said a little louder. Braxton barely reacted. James tried again.

"Braxton, could I talk to you for a second?"

Braxton looked up but didn't lower the music.

"Braxton, I don't mind if you listen quietly, but I can't have you disrupt the whole class. Could you please turn it down a little?"

Braxton glared at James and didn't turn down the music.

"Look—I'm going to have to call security if you don't turn it down. Could you please turn the music down so I don't have to do that?"

Braxton turned the music down, and James headed back to the portable blackboard to continue with the lesson, but the murmur of student voices behind him told him something was wrong. When he turned around, it was to face Braxton Young, who had gotten up from his seat to confront James in an uncomfortably close stare down at the front of the class—and with a threat.

"You better watch it—or you're gonna get hit!"

James could shrug off just about any amount of obnoxiousness directed his way but not a physical threat, and James responded proportionately. Security was immediately called, and Braxton was removed from the classroom. James distributed his work sheets and spent the rest of the class putting together a very detailed incident report for the school. After class, James took the additional step of filling out a police report.

Filing an official police report in addition to the incident report seemed appropriate to James as he wanted the threat on record on the off-chance Braxton actually tried to attack him someday. This was a fairly straightforward process as Earl Warren had a small school security office on the ground floor where NYC police officers were stationed.

James was, however, a little taken aback at how dismissive the police were about the incident—one officer actually discouraging James from filling out the report at all, muttering under his breath something about disgruntled teachers "blowing things out of proportion."

James would have confronted the police officer himself, but Dean Emerson, who apparently spent a lot of his time hanging around the security office and who had overheard everything, did it for him.

"You got it all wrong. This is that kid Braxton Young. We got two other incidents just like this one."

The last thing James wanted was help from Dick Emerson, but it made him feel better to know there were others who could back up his story. The police officer didn't seem overly impressed as he shrugged his shoulders and did his best to avoid eye contact with Dean Dick.

"It don't matter. He's a minor. Nothin' we can really do… Unless he actually assaults you—then maybe."

For all of Dean Emerson's misplaced zeal, there really wasn't, to James's surprise, anything he or the school could do either. James had expected Braxton to be immediately suspended, but suspending a student from public school was not an easy thing, as Braxton had a right to his public education and such rights are not taken away easily.

"We could go for a short-term suspension of a couple of days, but that might make things worse. I'd rather work on trying to get a superintendent's suspension, which would take him out of your class for good," Dick Emerson said as he gave James a reassuring pat on the back.

It was outrageous to James that there wasn't a better process to protect the safety of teachers—or of students for that matter. And James realized that day just how precarious the security situation was—and again made a mental note to find out more about school safety at Earl Warren.

The next day, Braxton was back in class as if nothing had happened. And neither James nor the other two teachers Braxton threatened would get any support from the school, the police, or the board of education as they dealt with Braxton Young and his potentially dangerous behavioral issues in their classes… for the next two months.

Although his own personal safety was certainly a concern, what the incident with Braxton had taught James was that in the classroom, he was on his own—and that in order to survive he would sometimes have to keep his head down and hope for the best. He avoided eye contact with Braxton, Keisha, or any of his other problem kids, pretending to look at the clock or at a textbook while sneaking a glance to see what they were up to. And if anyone was being particularly disruptive, James would usually just roll his eyes and overlook it as best he could while silently praying nobody important would notice so he wouldn't get yelled at—or even fired.

But the main impact on James was that he now knew he wasn't going to help Braxton or Keisha or many of his other students. A lot of his kids, particularly in his problem morning class, were beyond his help. He knew that now. And making the effort to help them would sacrifice what education he could offer to his other students—and maybe even get him beaten up for his trouble.

James's fantasies about changing the system or the school or even helping change the majority of the lives of his students had run into the brick wall of reality, and he found it increasingly difficult to maintain the energy and creativity he had brought to his classes at the beginning of the term.

"Oh, honey! Come on—it's time to get up and help make the world a better place!" Sue extolled James as she playfully tried to push him out of bed after the alarm had gone off for the third time one Monday morning.

James just moaned, his hands over his face and eyes.

"James!" Sue commanded as she shook him by the shoulders.

After what seemed like an eternity, the alarm stopped. *Sue must have mercifully turned it off*, James surmised. *Maybe he could call in sick*, James thought as he lay on his back with his eyes still closed.

James felt Sue's fingers running through his thick hair, which always took away any stress or worry and always made him smile. He opened his eyes to see Sue looking down at him through her frizzy morning hair with a mixture of love and concern.

"That Braxton kid really got to you."

"He didn't help."

"Look... I know everyone in the program had these really big plans and all... but I think you need to change your expectations a little. Like that teacher you're working with said..."

"Leslie."

"Didn't she tell you it's about changing the lives of just a couple of students? Why not just focus on one. That kid Jimmy... the one who never had a birthday party. What's his last name?

"Wiggins. Jimmy Wiggins."

"That poor little boy. Maybe he's the one kid you can help—the one that will make you get up in the morning, which you're going to do right now or you'll be late to school, young man!" Sue ordered as she pushed James out of bed.

As James stood outside Earl Warren that Monday morning, he took a deep breath as he psyched himself up for another week of classes. And James promised himself he would take Sue's and Leslie's advice—just focus on kids he could help—and in particular on Jimmy Wiggins. Perhaps Jimmy Wiggins was the one kid James could really help this year—the one kid that would make getting up in the morning easier—the one success story that would make his newfound profession worth all the sacrifice.

CHAPTER 13

TEACHER POLITICS AND TEACHING HISTORY

Teacher evaluations began several weeks into the first term, and while all teachers were evaluated, the process was only high stakes for new, untenured teachers. Tenured teachers almost always got satisfactory ratings, often irrespective of their actual performance as James had observed that summer.

This was not, however, the case for new teachers. If an untenured teacher received three unsatisfactory evaluations, they would be let go at the end of the year.

Fortunately for James, Kevin never evaluated his performance in his morning class in room 237. If he had, James's teaching career might very well have ended early. Instead, Kevin evaluated James's midmorning class with all the future honors students that always went well.

Informally, Kevin's comment to James during his first evaluation conference was that his lesson was one he would expect from a teacher with many more years of experience. Formally, Kevin informed James that the politics of the evaluation process dictated that he would have to find something wrong with his lesson plan that he could improve for next time.

James suggested that it could have been more creative, honestly believing creativity was something he needed to work on. Kevin disagreed.

"Take my advice and don't think too far out of the box, James. I'll put down that you could work a bit on time management and leave it at that," Kevin said as he made a few notes and checked off the "satisfactory" box on James's evaluation sheet.

James left his evaluation puzzled and with mixed emotions. His best teachers had always been creative people who had put a lot of time and effort into making their lessons fun in addition to being substantive. Surely creativity should count for something in the evaluation process.

Apparently it did—and not always in a good way—at least according to Robert Sullivan's assistant principal who, to James's shock, had elected to give Robert an "unsatisfactory" for his first evaluation. Ironically, Robert had thought his classes were going pretty well—his students appreciating his sense of humor and originality.

"It's complete bullshit," Robert said a bit too loudly as he played with the ridiculously large order of uneaten french fries that accompanied the massive cheeseburger in front of him during a hastily arranged lunch at the neighborhood diner.

James could find nothing wrong with Robert's rather insightful lesson plan covering some of the poems of Maya Angelou.

"We just never got along," Robert said of his assistant principal.

"She's always disliked me—especially after she found out I went to Yale."

As Robert explained, his AP, a slightly disheveled, middle-aged woman by the name of Mellissa McDonald, had had her heart set on going to Yale back in the day but had been turned down—twice. And as Yale had broken her heart, she was determined to get her revenge on one of its graduates.

James thought the whole thing rather silly and suggested that Robert find out exactly what his AP expected of him and to be sure to put that into his next evaluated lesson—even if it meant doing something more traditional.

Robert stared down at his uneaten lunch, shaking his head. "Waste of food. I'm already making a list of private schools to apply to. It's a personal thing with her—she's not going to let me stay in the system."

And Robert turned out to be right.

No matter what Robert did, Mellissa McDonald refused to check the "satisfactory" box on Robert's evaluations, and he would eventually be forced out of the Teaching Fellows program and the public school system.

The frustrating irony for James was that Robert was the second teaching fellow the system had done away with who was, objectively, a better teacher than he was. The system's standardized tests had gotten rid of Martin King, one of the best teachers James had ever seen, and personal politics, it seemed, had gotten rid of Robert Sullivan.

"It'll be fun. I won't get to change the world, but I'll get to coach wrestling and teach history instead of English," Robert said with a sigh.

Ironically, private schools did not require a master's degree or state certification to teach and weren't beholden to the board of education's restrictive rules on who could teach what—and, counterintuitively, those less stringent requirements resulted in teaching quality that was almost always excellent.

The prerequisites for state certification to teach in public school, in contrast, were labyrinthine.

James had once seen all the nonsensical hoops the system made a person jump through represented as a large flowchart that resembled a complex engineering project he was only barely able to follow, and the quality of teachers that were eventually strained through was decidedly scattershot.

James wondered if all the absurd requirements actually drove good people away from the system as it had with Robert and Martin, while actually encouraging the mediocre and the downright untalented who would put up with all the nonsense in exchange for lifetime employment in positions they could never have obtained based on their respective talents alone.

And there were many instances when James would wonder out loud what, if anything, many of those "certified" teachers were teaching their kids.

Like Robert, James had always wanted to teach history and political science—but unless he chose to teach at a private school, he would never get the chance to teach a subject other than English, due to his undergraduate major (his law school education notwithstanding)—at least not officially.

Unofficially, James would end up teaching a lot of history, as well as science, geography, economics, and even occasionally mathematics. This was because nearly all James's students—even many of his smarter kids— were astonishingly uneducated.

James would continually be surprised and aghast at the basic knowledge his students lacked—basic facts about the world: history, geography, elementary science and math, American government—even basic facts about their own cultural heritage. They often seemed to rely upon movies and television for their education—not books—not parents—and, apparently, not public school.

And it was more than just not knowing things James had previously assumed were common knowledge. It was a lack of a sense of time and place in the world—a world the majority of his kids accepted the way it was—and assumed had been pretty much the same throughout most of human history.

One of James's students in a class in late November, just before the Thanksgiving break, expressed confusion as to why the Pilgrims hadn't just flown over from England. To James's shock, many of the other students in the class considered the question to be a good one, although a few seemed to understand that airplanes hadn't been invented yet—which prompted the student to ask, "Why didn't they just drive then?"

Another class had no problem with the idea that there was electricity back in Shakespeare's day—prompting James to ask a bit too cynically if the students thought Shakespeare had cable TV—to which one student replied, "Probably."

The student was quickly corrected—not by James—but by another student.

"That can't be right. My grandma once told me that a long time ago there wasn't cable and you could only get four or five good channels. And since Shakespeare is older than my grandma, he probably only had the regular TV."

This prompted an earnest class discussion, which James watched—slack-jawed—about how hard life was back in olden times when people had only five channels on their televisions and no pay-per-view.

In another class when introducing the poetry of Langston Hughes, James had thought it appropriate to have a discussion of the history of civil rights for African Americans after the Civil War but before the civil rights movement so they could better understand what Langston Hughes was writing about.

The only problem was that almost no one in the class had heard of the Civil War. Indeed, many students believed there had been slavery in America at the time Langston Hughes was writing and that it had been ended by Martin Luther King somehow.

Needless to say, James postponed his lesson on Langston Hughes that day and substituted an impromptu lesson in basic American history—which seemed to be going well until his discussion of President Lincoln and the Emancipation Proclamation. The problem was his students weren't quite sure who President Lincoln was.

"He's on the five-dollar bill and the penny," James said, holding his breath as he waited for someone to respond.

After a long, awkward silence, it slowly dawned on Deon Jefferson, a likable kid who sat in the front row and generally paid attention that he did, indeed, know who President Lincoln was.

"Oh yeah. I heard of him. He the dude who got shot."

"That's right," James said, exhaling audibly.

"I saw a show on TV about him. They shot him in the head."

"Yes. Lincoln was shot in the head—assassinated," James confirmed, nodding his head vigorously.

"Yeah—that was sad. They never shoulda put that dude in a convertible."

The real tragedy was that nobody in the class laughed.

CHAPTER 14

JIMMY'S BIRTHDAY PARTY

James was running late the Friday morning of Jimmy Wiggins's birthday. So when he noticed "Jimmy's birthday party" penciled in on his calendar, his first instinct was that maybe he should just blow it off. Jimmy Wiggins's attendance was becoming more and more erratic, so there was a good chance Jimmy wouldn't even be there that day.

On the other hand, Jimmy could be that one kid James could really have an impact on that year. The revelation that Jimmy Wiggins had never had a birthday party in all his childhood was something that had really stuck with James—and James had sworn to himself that he would give Jimmy at least one small birthday party while Jimmy still had a childhood.

And Jimmy was a good kid, always polite and respectful—but slipping away—evident to James, not just because of his ever more unpredictable attendance but because of his deteriorating appearance and general demeanor, which was becoming increasingly distant with every passing week.

James was worried about him.

He had tried several times to contact Jimmy's parents—but neither he nor the school were able to contact anybody, which was not surprising considering there wasn't anyone in Jimmy's life who cared enough to give the kid even one lousy birthday party during Jimmy's fourteen years of rapidly vanishing childhood.

Yes, Leslie's mantra that a successful teaching career meant changing the lives of just a few students definitely applied here.

If James could reach Jimmy by doing a little something special for him—by throwing him a small birthday party at the end of class—he could inspire Jimmy Wiggins to come to school more often or at the very least give him a happy memory of something every child should have happy memories of.

Besides, James knew Sue would kill him if she ever found out he'd blown it off.

So James made a mad dash to the supermarket that morning and bought some cupcakes—mostly chocolate because one of the few things he knew about Jimmy Wiggins was that chocolate cake was his favorite food—along with some festive plates and napkins. It wasn't much—but hopefully it was enough—and hopefully Jimmy Wiggins would come to school that day.

As the start of the last period of the day—and the week—approached, James collected the cupcakes he had stored in the office and trotted up the stairs, flying past several winded teenagers along the way, to his final class of the day. But as his students sauntered in, James was dismayed to see Jimmy Wiggins's seat empty.

As he took attendance, he wondered to himself whether he should save the cupcakes for another day—or if the idea of having a birthday party for Jimmy was just a silly one after all. But just as James got to the bottom of the attendance list and was about to mark Jimmy Wiggins absent for yet another class, Jimmy, a little out of breath from his climb up the stairs, came panting through the classroom door, giving James a guilty half smile for being late, and took his seat in the back of the room.

James began the class as usual—his plan to reserve the last fifteen minutes for cupcakes and a round of "Happy Birthday." Jimmy also began the class as he usually did—quietly settling into his seat and reverting to the sort of dazed look on his face—the dead look in his eyes—that had become the norm for Jimmy Wiggins and that had become so concerning for James.

Over the course of the term, James had tried unsuccessfully to engage Jimmy in class—calling on him to answer a question or to read out loud whenever it seemed as if Jimmy had tuned out for the day. Most of the time Jimmy would just shrug and indicate that he couldn't answer James's questions or dutifully perform whatever task James gave him without energy or interest, only to revert to the tired-of-life stare that no fourteen-year-old should ever have. Perhaps today would be different, James hoped.

James finished his lesson early as planned and with a faint smile, faced the class.

"So… I've ended class a little early today because we have a birthday to celebrate," James revealed as he turned his attention to Jimmy.

James had expected Jimmy to react, but he didn't—continuing his dull gaze into space. James tried again. "Jimmy, I believe you are turning fifteen today. Happy birthday, Jimmy!"

Jimmy's expression turned to one of bewilderment, and James wondered if, perhaps, he had gotten the date wrong somehow.

"It is your birthday today, Jimmy, isn't it?"

Jimmy was slow to answer—but his brow was furrowed now—always a good indicator to James that he had succeeded in getting Jimmy's attention. Jimmy cocked his head to one side, as if not really being able to comprehend what was happening but then slowly answered James's question with a faint but growing smile.

"Yes, mister. Today is my birthday. I'd forgotten."

"Well… I believe you once told me chocolate cake was your favorite food…" James reminded Jimmy as he produced the boxes of cupcakes, which got the attention of the class more quickly than he had ever believed possible.

"Happy birthday, Jimmy!" James repeated.

"Happy birthday, Jimmy!" the class repeated in very loud, enthusiastic unison—so unexpected that James's startle reflex nearly caused him to drop the cupcakes.

The amount of energy the class was suddenly expending at the end of the day—particularly on a Friday—was something James hadn't seen before. But then it dawned on James—the class understood Jimmy's situation better than he or any teacher or administrator ever could. James's students understood that this party was more than just cupcakes and a kind gesture. They understood that this birthday party was something Jimmy Wiggins desperately needed as a human being.

Jimmy was a kid on the brink who wasn't being cared for—and who needed some acknowledgment that someone did actually care about him. And as James passed out the plates, napkins, and cupcakes—as he watched Jimmy's smile slowly broaden—it occurred to James that he hadn't really ever seen Jimmy Wiggins smile before and that this was probably the first time Jimmy had sported a genuine smile in quite some time. And his smile was wide and infectious, but sadly jagged, James noted—with many stained teeth which had probably received even less attention over the course of their existence than Jimmy had.

"I'm afraid I don't have any candles—but I think a round of 'Happy Birthday' is in order," James announced with a certain degree of trepidation as James, unlike many people who enjoy singing in public, knew he couldn't carry a tune and refrained from doing so whenever possible.

"I'll start it," Danielle Williams chimed in as James gave a sigh of relief.

As the class sang "Happy Birthday" to Jimmy, James was happy see Jimmy enjoying himself, but what impressed him most was the reaction of the class—that the instinct to help another human being existed within every one of his students and that this instinct triumphed over everything else that was going on in their complicated lives.

"That's a really nice thing you did, Mr. Hartman," Danielle said between cupcake bites, looking up at James with frosting-encrusted lips and an expression of earnest contentment.

James saw an opportunity.

"Hey Danielle…" James hesitated.

Danielle looked up at James questioningly.

James would normally have never discussed one student's situation with another and felt uncomfortable doing so. But in Jimmy's case, James had exhausted his options within the system and needed to do something, so he continued.

"Do you know what Jimmy's story is? I've tried calling his parents but…"

Danielle's expression turned uncharacteristically cheerless as she looked over toward Jimmy, who was enjoying his birthday cupcake along with several other students. She turned back to face James.

"You ain't gonna find no parents to talk to, mister. I don't know the whole story, but Jimmy—he been through a lot… and he just don't care no more."

James didn't think it appropriate to probe further and simply nodded to Danielle in acknowledgment. He had never seen melancholy in his reliably ebullient student, and James concluded that things with Jimmy Wiggins were even worse than he had feared. But he had tried calling home and he had brought Jimmy to the attention of school officials… What else could James do?

"Hey! Mr. Hartman!" Danielle exclaimed, pointing at him accusingly with her half-eaten cupcake.

James's thoughts were scattered like fallen leaves in the wind. What had he done now?

"You didn't correct my double-negatives! I just used two of them!"

James smiled. "You're right. But I got you to correct them yourself, didn't I?"

Danielle gave James a friendly smirk in reply before taking another bite of cupcake and rejoining her friends who were busily skirmishing over the last of the cupcakes.

As the class, the day, and the week came to an end, James noticed Principal White curiously observing Jimmy Wiggins's birthday party through the window of the classroom door. He waived to her, but his waive was greeted with only a polite smile back, and then Principal White was gone.

The bell rang, and the party was suddenly over as students scrambled for the door to begin their weekend break. Jimmy Wiggins quietly thanked James on his way out—and then he was gone as well, and James was left to clean up the used plates, napkins, and fragments of cupcakes that now littered the room.

As James cleaned up, he congratulated himself on accomplishing a lot that afternoon. He had given a boy in need a small but meaningful gift and in doing so had earned the trust of his students. Perhaps Jimmy would be motivated to come to class more consistently. Perhaps it would even give him a little hope. Perhaps even the small things can have a profound impact. And perhaps this would be the case with the little birthday party at the end of class James had given to Jimmy Wiggins.

CHAPTER 15

THE MONDAY AFTER

James was still feeling proud of himself the Monday after Jimmy Wiggins's birthday party. Sue had gotten teary-eyed when James told her the story—which was kind of embarrassing and far too emotional a reaction as far as James was concerned.

"I'm sure he'll remember what you did for him for many years to come," Sue assured James through her tears.

The Monday after Jimmy's birthday party proceeded as usual—a crappy first class with lots of work sheets and the occasional outburst from Keisha Sanders and company—and midmorning and afternoon classes that went well although not without a little drama from Danielle Williams after James returned the "Gift of the Magi" papers.

Predictably, all the papers needed a lot of revision, and James had his students rewrite them using his corrections and comments for a better grade. He had given the majority of the papers a grade of C, which the class wasn't thrilled about but which was actually quite generous in James's mind.

Although James was beholden to Kevin and the system for final grades, grades for individual assignments were entirely within James's discretion as far as he could tell, and James thought it important that his students have an honest assessment of their work so they could actually improve their writing.

Most of the class grudgingly accepted their marks with the promise of a better grade after they revised the assignment.

"You gave me a B?" Danielle stated in a shaky voice as she confronted James after class.

James had actually given Danielle a B+, which was the highest grade in the class.

"You gave me a B, mister?" Danielle repeated, her hands clutching the graded paper, shaking.

"It's a B+ actually..."

"It don't matter! It still a B, and I don't get no B grades, mister!"

"I think if you look at the corrections..."

"Ain't no teacher ever give me no B grade, mister!" Danielle informed James as she tried to conceal a tear dripping down the side of her cheek.

And James suddenly realized that Danielle had never had a teacher give her an honest assessment of her work before.

Although Danielle was the best student in the class, her writing was still riddled with mistakes. Some were easily correctable grammatical errors—some were because Danielle hadn't proofread her work as well as she was capable of doing. Earlier intervention for a smart, hardworking kid like Danielle would have produced a student on track to go to a good four-year college. Now Danielle would have to work hard to overcome her deficiencies in English to be on that track, which given Danielle's personality and intelligence, James was confident she could achieve.

But what if Danielle had gone through high school without an honest appraisal of her work or if she hadn't been as smart or dedicated? James could only imagine that Danielle's former teachers were either too lazy or too incompetent to actually read and correct her assignments. And with grade inflation combined with the pressure to appease students, parents, and school administrators, perhaps even competent teachers would look the other way and award high grades for work that was, objectively, average or even below.

As James sat down with Danielle and went over her paper—and Danielle actually digested all the corrections—Danielle's anger slowly melted into a kind of sadness.

"You right, mister. This ain't... isn't very good, is it?" Danielle concluded with a sigh.

"It isn't too bad. You've got the right structure, and the content is good. You just need to work on correcting a few grammatical bad habits is all."

"Why none of my teachers ever told me about things like run-on sentences and sentence fragments and shit like— Stuff like that?"

James didn't have an answer. Danielle nodded her head and gave James a faint smile.

"Thanks, mister. I'll work on this and bring it back next week." Danielle paused for a moment at the door before leaving and looked back at James questioningly.

"Hey, mister? Do you think I'll be able to be a doctor someday?"

This was the first time James had ever seen Danielle unsure about anything—let alone her life's dream, and he hoped that whatever came out of his mouth would strike the right balance between encouragement and honesty.

"It's still possible... But the honest answer is that it will be a long and difficult road."

Danielle thought for a moment and nodded to herself as she digested James's answer.

"Thanks, mister."

As James headed for the English department office, he again felt a sense of accomplishment as he did after Jimmy Wiggins's birthday party. He was, by being a good teacher, being honest with Danielle and helping her achieve her goal of going to college. Perhaps in some small way James was, as a teacher at an underperforming public high school, helping to change the world for the better.

"Hartman! In my office!" Kevin commanded, pointing to his office door.

Kevin looked particularly pissed off, and James knew immediately that he had done something very wrong.

"Have a seat."

James sat. Kevin didn't.

"Look, James, I can't have you breaking school rules whenever you want."

James didn't immediately know what school rules Kevin was referring to.

"Principal White has a very strict rule against food in the classrooms—and especially against birthday parties during class—you can't have them... ever! It's one of her pet peeves."

"Oh that," James said with a sigh of relief.

James had thought for a moment that his late afternoon snacks had been discovered and that he would have to discontinue his extremely successful solution to the school's insane ten-thirty-a.m. lunch policy. But Kevin's tone indicated that Jimmy's birthday party was more than a trivial infraction.

"Principal White really chewed me out this morning over your Friday afternoon class, James. I just can't have you doing stuff like that anymore."

"Look, Kevin..."

"I don't care what your excuse is. The next infraction goes in your file. Understand?"

Putting something in your "file" was the ultimate threat to a teacher as there was, apparently, a file of the Orwellian variety kept somewhere deep within the bowels of the board of education bureaucracy that contained a record of everything a teacher ever did wrong in their career.

James's indifference to the mention of his hallowed "file" seemed to upset Kevin even more.

"I don't think you quite understand…" Kevin's face was turning red.

"Look, Kevin. I don't intend to have any more birthday parties in class—and I certainly apologize for breaking the rule. But this was a unique case where a student of mine had never had a birthday party before. I thought it was appropriate to give him one—and if that has to go in my file, so be it." James held his hands up in surrender.

James understood that Kevin had the power to end his teaching career all by himself—that he could manipulate the evaluation process and simply judge him to be an unsatisfactory teacher, as had happened to his friend Robert Sullivan. But he also felt it was inappropriate to kiss Kevin's ass over a ridiculous rule that he was perfectly justified in breaking.

Kevin stammered a bit, seeming to begrudgingly understand—perhaps even admiring James's resolve, James hoped.

"Okay. Well… Look on the bright side. At least you had sense enough not to have birthday candles. That would have been a fire hazard, and we would have both been in trouble."

James smiled and nodded. It had been purely by accident that James had forgotten the birthday candles.

Leslie had a few choice adjectives for Principal White and Kevin Newcomb—including a few in Klingon—after James told her the story over yet another drink at the Starving Writer that James actually did finish.

"You can't just follow the rules and be a good teacher, Jim. Here's to not just 'covering your ass!'" Leslie toasted with her third drink of the late afternoon and looked admiringly at James.

"I'll bet it does him some good, your little birthday party. Maybe Jimmy Wiggins is that one person you'll really help this year that'll make it all worthwhile. I'll bet he comes to class more often now," Leslie said with a wink.

Unfortunately, Leslie would lose that bet.

Jimmy Wiggins's appearance, demeanor, and most disturbingly, body odor would deteriorate along with his attendance until, finally, Jimmy Wiggins would disappear from Earl Warren altogether. And despite inquiries by the school and by James, his whereabouts and his fate would remain a mystery for quite some time to come.

CHAPTER 16

PARENT-TEACHER CONFERENCES
AND STREET GANGS

Kevin became a real pain in the ass the week of parent-teacher conferences.

James thought that the pressure coming from Principal White must have been pretty intense, and as the week before parent-teacher conferences progressed, everyone was feeling slightly on edge as Principal White's many dictates filtered their way down through the administration to the faculty.

There were constant reminders from Kevin—again and again—about the procedures that needed to be followed, the way the classrooms needed to look, and that everyone should be formally dressed for the occasion.

The classrooms and the hallways were tidied up for the first time since the beginning of the term. Educational posters were plastered anywhere there was blank wall space, and as much student work as possible was put on display.

The process reminded James about a film he had seen in a freshman psychology class about the infamous Stanford Prison Experiment where the horrible conditions of the student-run prison were covered up in order to impress—or more accurately to fool—their visiting family members.

James's students' reaction was decidedly cynical.

"Why can't they make the school pretty all the time, mister?" was Danielle's pointed question to James. James shrugged and rolled his eyes.

All the effort would have been harmless enough if it weren't helping to further mask a serious problem at Earl Warren that was being ignored even more than it usually was—the presence of street gangs at the school.

Sometimes gang members were present in the building itself. Sometimes gang members would assemble outside, waiting for kids after school. And street gangs generally had a large influence on the students in their own neighborhoods—sometimes by recruiting them into their ranks and encouraging them to drop out of school and sometimes by intimidating or using physical violence against kids who didn't join.

The issue wasn't whether street gangs existed—they did—and everyone from Principal White to the police to the school's janitorial staff knew it. The problem was that the world of street gangs was a murky one and no one ever had specifics. At meetings, faculty would occasionally complain passionately about the lack of concern the school and the police seemed to have for the problem—only to be answered frustratingly by Principal White in her signature monotone that she needed names and that everything else was "just rumors."

The kids always knew what was going on.

And the faculty, unless they were completely tone deaf to their students, would get wind that there was some kind of gang activity happening on a given day because their kids, even the better students, wouldn't be able to concentrate, and the tension level would rise dramatically in anticipation of whatever violence was scheduled to happen.

There was a constant fear of "getting jumped," but other than that, students weren't willing to talk about it—perhaps correctly sensing that nobody at the school could or would help them and that being labeled a snitch could be hazardous to one's health.

As luck would have it, classes began to noticeably deteriorate during the week before parent-teacher conferences. As a new teacher, James didn't understand what was going on at first until Leslie explained to him that the word was out that something was going to happen at the end of the week—although nobody knew quite what.

That Friday, attendance was noticeably lower than usual, and what was left of James's classes were almost unteachable. James got an unambiguous warning from, of all people, Maria Rodriguez in his midmorning class, who had been uncharacteristically quiet and distant that day. After class, Maria stayed behind, waiting for the last student to leave before approaching James.

"You take the subway, mister?" Maria quietly asked.

James did take the number one train along with many of his students for one stop where he and his students would part ways—his students transferring to the number two and three trains to the Bronx and James continuing uptown to his apartment on the Upper West Side near Columbia University.

Maria quickly looked around to make sure no one was listening.

"Don't take it today."

James was left wondering what he was supposed to do next. Maria Rodriguez had given him specific information about where and when something was going to happen—and because Maria was indisputably trustworthy, he decided he needed to report it.

James went to the security office where he found Dick Emerson jabbering at a weary-looking police officer who was doing a very poor job at pretending to listen.

"Excuse me… Dick…," James said, with as friendly a smile as he could muster.

James hated using the nickname "Dick," but Dick Emerson had insisted.

"What can I do you for, Mr. Hartman?"

"I don't quite know how to report this, but I just had a student tell me something was going to happen on the subway today after school."

"You have anything else?" Dean Emerson asked nonchalantly.

"Not really. But I heard it from Maria Rodriguez. She's a straight-A student in my class, and she's not the type of person that would tell me something like that if it weren't true."

To James's surprise, his story succeeded in eliciting a small amount of interest from the jaded police officer, who went out of his way to assure James that the police were aware of the situation and were "monitoring it."

After school, James was tempted to take Maria's advice and not take the subway home. But it was raining that day, and James assumed that the police had everything under control.

At first everything seemed pretty normal as James took a seat across from some uncharacteristically apprehensive-looking Earl Warren students. Danielle Williams followed into the subway car soon after, but when she saw James, a worried look came over her face.

"Mister, I don't think you should be here today..."

Danielle and James turned to face the growing chorus of yelling and screaming that was quickly attracting the attention of everyone on the train. Throngs of teenagers were jumping the turnstiles and flooding the station platform with a revel of failing arms and swinging fists as fights broke out all over the platform.

The train just sat in the station—doors open—with its passengers powerless to do anything other than watch the orgy of violence taking place outside and pray it didn't spill over into the train itself.

An army of police officers followed almost immediately after, also jumping the turnstiles and flooding through the emergency exits, their blue uniforms amalgamating into the fighting mass of teenagers for a short time as they slowly sorted the bedlam into the handcuffed, who were seated in a long row at one end of the platform, and the rest, who scattered and ran away.

After about ten minutes, it was over. Danielle turned to James, who couldn't conceal the discouraged look on his face.

"Were you scared, mister?" Danielle asked.

James shook his head "no."

James hadn't really been scared. But the incident had made him more pessimistic about how much faculty and administration could really do for kids who were faced with so many obstacles in their lives like street gangs and dangerous neighborhoods and family issues and poverty and the many other impediments that people like himself who lived outside their world could never really understand.

Danielle studied James's expression.

"Yeah, Mr. Hartman. It's really sad, isn't it?"

By Monday everything was pretty much back to normal, except that James decided to dress more formally in a suit and tie for parent-teacher conferences, to the great amusement of his students who had thought his usual dress of khaki pants, a dress shirt, and a tie *was* formal attire.

Indeed, his students expressed surprise when James explained to them that he could have actually dressed even more formally, having left his really nice three-thousand-dollar suit at home. There was unusual interest, even from some of the more quiet students in James's classes, about how they should dress for a job interview.

And James suddenly understood that, in the same way many of his students lacked a basic knowledge of higher education, the majority of his students had absolutely no idea about how to dress for a formal interview— and the ensuing class conversations James had about the importance of appearance in interviews and in the workplace generally were some of the most productive and useful that James had ever had with his students.

This brought up in James's mind the issue of school uniforms.

Public schools in New York didn't require them, although James remembered the impassioned support for school uniforms that had been made by Joseph Biles during his hated presentation to the teaching fellows over the summer—a sentiment that the more progressive members of his cohort flatly rejected as just another rule in a system that had too many rules and one that would stifle the individuality and self-expression of its students.

But James was beginning to agree with Joseph Biles.

Aside from teaching students something about formal dress and eliminating student competition in this area, school uniforms might have helped with the gang problem James had recently witnessed and, by standardizing student dress, possibly lessened the long lines for the security scanning machines the students had to endure every morning.

Leslie agreed with James's assessment but doubted uniforms would ever be required as the issue was, like the issue of having more vocational training in public schools, "too politically sensitive."

After school, the faculty went to their assigned classrooms to prep for parent-teacher conferences. James was a little nervous—particularly at the prospect of meeting either Braxton's or Keisha's parents. He needn't have been.

James sat. And he sat. And he sat.

Over the course of the evening, James's sign-in sheet slowly collected a few names—but only the parents of James's best students—parents James didn't really need to see. Danielle's mother showed up with a very nervous Danielle in tow. James was struck by how young Danielle's mother was—as young as he was and with a teenage daughter to take care of all by herself.

"I wanted to talk to you about Danielle's recent paper," Danielle's mother said in a shaky voice as she produced the "Gift of the Magi" paper with James's numerous corrections.

"Yes. Danielle and I went over the corrections and she rewrote..."

"Yes, I know. But I want to make sure her grades ain't slippin' in your class. I want Danielle to go to college someday."

"I do too. And when she goes, I want to make sure she's prepared so that she succeeds once she gets there."

Danielle's mother seemed to relax a little.

"So her grades ain't slippin' then? And she ain't causing you no trouble...?"

"Danielle's the best student in the class— I wish I had a whole class full of students like your daughter, Mrs. Williams."

Danielle stole a quick, nervous glance toward her mother, who exhaled audibly as though she had been holding her breath the entire time.

James felt even more certain after meeting Danielle's mother that Danielle would make it to college someday.

James's hopes for nearly all his other students were dimmed after parent-teacher conferences however. Their parents—the people in his students' lives who were ultimately the most responsible for their success or failure—didn't think student-teacher conferences important enough to show up even when their kids were failing.

And at the end of the evening, out of all the parents of all the children in James's overly crowded classes, just twelve put their signatures on James's sign-in sheet. James was depressed. Catherine Angel was jealous.

"Wow, James! You're popular! I only got six."

Leslie had done a little better with fourteen. The other teaching fellows had numbers similar to James's, and Norman Griffin had just one parent show up.

As James swam laps at the YMCA later that evening, he thought about all the challenges his kids faced. He wondered, as he efficiently cut through the water on his nightly four-thousand-yard swim to nowhere, how he or anyone else was going to be able to help those kids when too often their biggest challenge was having parents—often lacking in education themselves—who didn't consider it important to show up to parent-teacher conferences.

CHAPTER 17

THE TRIAL

Leslie's strategies for dealing with the disarray that was James's first-period class in the dreaded room 237, though not perfect solutions, had, over time, calmed things down to the point that someone looking in wouldn't be confused as to whether they were seeing an English class or a rumpus room—and to the point that some of the better students were actually producing some meaningful work.

Keisha Sanders and Braxton Young were still James's biggest behavioral challenges, but the constant barrage of work sheets at least gave them some paper they could doodle on as they pretended to complete their assignments. James still occasionally made attempts to help them with their work out of a sense of duty, even though he knew full well the effort would be counterproductive.

"Why you care, mister?" was Keisha's usual retort.

And James was content to let her go back to quietly gossiping with her friends in the back of the room—an unsatisfying compromise—but one that gave the other students a chance to have some sort of an English class that term.

Braxton would usually just ignore James as he sketched while quietly listening to his music—another reluctant but effective compromise that Braxton seemed to be sticking to. Or Braxton might ask for a new handout so he could create another drawing on the back of it—often of sneakers of one brand or another, which was something Braxton and many of the other boys in the class took a great interest in for reasons quite foreign to James, as he had been born with very little fashion sense.

Braxton was actually a fairly decent artist, and James often wondered if a kid like Braxton, who had no interest or ability in traditional academics, should be in a traditional high school at all—and lamented the dearth of art classes and other nonacademic offerings in the New York City public schools. Braxton's talents would almost certainly go undeveloped, and James wondered what a kid like Braxton—a kid almost certain to drop out of high school at the age of sixteen—would end up doing with his life.

Leslie's take on the issue, in one of the more politically charged conversations that had taken place at a recent Thursday after-school happy hour at the Starving Writer, was that public schools should go back to offering more vocational training.

"Nobody wants to admit that some kids aren't ever going to be college material. But heck— A good electrician or mechanic earns more than I do—and without student loans to worry about. But you can't ever bring up vocational training for those kids—it's become too politically incorrect," Leslie concluded as she ordered another of her beloved Jack Kerouac drink concoctions.

"Yeah, it's something everyone talks about privately, but there's too much resistance from all sides," Catherine agreed, sipping her usual Tennessee whiskey on the rocks.

At the time, James felt uncomfortable being a part of the conversation.

In James's world, pretty much everyone was on track to go to college—and a college education was assumed to be part of the American dream. It was also a part of James's mission and the mission of the Teaching Fellows program to make that dream available to everyone.

But James was beginning to see, as he studied Braxton's latest drawing of a pair of well-rendered Air Jordan high-tops that college really wasn't for everyone—certainly not Braxton Young—and that, perhaps, public schools would serve their students better if they offered more than just the college pathway to a successful and happy life.

Indeed, as James thought about his students that day, he realized that less than half of them—probably far less—could ever develop, at this stage in their lives, the academic skills to succeed at a four-year college even with the best high school education and lots of extra help that they weren't going to get at home or at school.

And this brought up another conflict for James. Should he concentrate on the top third of the class that had a chance at college and give up on students like Keisha and Braxton who were likely to drop out no matter what he did? Or should he make an effort to help everyone, which would mean giving less attention to students who had more of a chance of actually going to college and succeeding once they got there. Perhaps if there had been an earlier intervention for kids like Keisha and Braxton…

"Hartman!"

James's thoughts were scattered like dropped change. Dick Emerson had stuck his oversized balding head into the room, and his booming, heavily Brooklyn-accented command to attention had, again, needlessly disrupted one of James's classes.

"Could you come see me in the hallway for a second?"

"What have Mr. Hartman done now?" Keisha mockingly chimed in, which in this instance mirrored exactly what James was thinking to himself. What *had* he done to deserve another scolding from Dick Emerson?

James stepped into the hallway, fully expecting a lecture on rules and discipline, but the Dean Emerson who greeted James was unexpectedly giddy—an emotion he expressed with a sort of demonic exhilaration, making Dick Emerson appear to be even more of a dick than usual.

"Hartman, I've got some great news. We've got that kid Braxton that threatened you."

James looked over at Braxton, who was quietly sketching in the back of the class. James was confused. The incident with Braxton had occurred over six weeks ago, and nobody seemed to care at the time. More importantly, James and Braxton were enjoying a truce of sorts—and James didn't want to make things worse by pursuing it now.

"We got four more teachers he's threatened. That's enough that we can make the case he should get a superintendent's suspension. You'll have to come out to Brooklyn to testify at the hearing," Dean Emerson informed James, patting him on the shoulder.

Testify? James thought, shaking his head in disbelief as he stood watching Dean Dick disappear down the hallway with a bounce in his step.

James would learn upon further investigation that the legal procedure required to suspend a student from a New York City public school was very complex—almost Kafkaesque—which meant it would be quite difficult to suspend Braxton or any other student who had the wherewithal to contest such a suspension on procedural grounds—never mind any factual discrepancies that might arise. And James could see how such a system would unfairly penalize those students whose parents either didn't—or couldn't—advocate for their children themselves or whose parents couldn't afford professional representation.

And as a lawyer, James could also see the other side of the equation: how such a system would unfairly shield those students who deserved a suspension but knew how to manipulate the system.

But the real issue for James was how inefficient—and expensive— such a formal legal proceeding would be. There had to be a more streamlined way to deal with disruptive students that was both speedy and fair. Punishing Braxton for something he did nearly two months previously wouldn't change his behavior—and suspending him for an extended period of time would almost certainly do him—and ultimately society— more harm than good. There had to be a better way.

But despite his misgivings, James found himself obligated to testify at Braxton Young's hearing in Brooklyn the following Wednesday. Kevin wasn't happy about it because he had to arrange for a substitute teacher to cover all of James's classes for the day, but he didn't have any choice in the matter either.

The morning of "the trial," as James had jokingly referred to it all the previous week to Sue, who had become more than a little annoyed with James's sudden interest in the legal complexities of student suspensions, James, Dean Emerson, and the four other recipients of Braxton's physical threats headed out to Brooklyn where they would all give their sworn testimony.

As Dean Emerson excitedly prepped the group—yet again—during the subway ride to Brooklyn, James pretended to pay attention, actually wondering how such a complete idiot like Dick Emerson could be put in a position of responsibility and be given the title of Dean. And he prayed that, whatever the outcome of "the trial," Braxton wouldn't have another outburst in his morning class.

The procedure itself was confusing, even for someone with James's legal training. James had expected a formal hearing of some sort—but because Braxton's parents hadn't yet arrived, he was, instead, called into a closet-sized office to give sworn, recorded testimony in front of a woman who appeared to be an administrative judge.

James's affable comportment, inspired by sympathy for anyone in the legal profession relegated to working such a thankless job in such a cramped environment, wasn't returned—the judge apparently wanting to get James's interview over with as quickly as possible. So James dutifully answered the judge's questions about the incident with Braxton in the same, disinterested, mechanical tone in which they were asked.

The questions were inquisitorial in nature, designed to highlight possible inconsistencies between his testimony and his initial incident report. But James had been through enough depositions to understand the process and didn't feel offended by the questioning in the way the other teachers would later say they were.

What was offensive to James was the process itself.

As a student, James had always assumed teachers and administrators had a great deal of power to deal with disruptive behavior—and in his private high school that was certainly true. It wasn't as if there weren't students with behavioral issues in private school. James could think of several kids in his own high school class who had gotten expelled for both academic and behavioral reasons.

The difference was that the teachers and administrators at a private school could remove such a student whenever they needed to. And this threat of expulsion, combined with vastly smaller class sizes, greater parental involvement, and a considerably more motivated student body, meant there were almost never any serious issues with student conduct in such an environment.

In public school, the opposite was true. Teachers and administrators had almost no power to discipline or remove students no matter how disruptive—or even dangerous. James understood that students had a right to a public education and strongly supported that right. But didn't the other students in the class also have that right? And wasn't a student like Braxton Young taking that right away from them?

James knew that many would blame Braxton's teachers and the school for not effectively dealing with Braxton's behavioral issues. They would say his teachers didn't teach him in the right way and that the school didn't provide enough remedial help and support. And such an assessment would be easy to make because Braxton was still a child and children can't be blamed for such things. And although reasonable sounding, such an assessment couldn't have been further from the truth in Braxton's case.

The truth was that the school had tried to intervene in the ways that it could, but nothing had worked. His teachers had tried to teach him, but they had been threatened with physical violence when they did. And perhaps most crucially, Braxton's parents didn't seem capable of—or very interested in—dealing with either his behavioral problems or his academic failures.

There had to be a better procedure for dealing with disruptive students—and there certainly had to be better alternatives to a long suspension, which, at best, would result in Braxton staying home and watching television for a few weeks.

But in the end, it didn't matter.

As it turned out, Braxton's parents never showed up for the hearing, which meant the whole thing was canceled. Dick Emerson was visibly sullen on the way back from Brooklyn and would spend the rest of the afternoon viciously berating as many students and teachers as he could find in an effort to combat his depressed mood.

James stayed out of his way.

As it turned out, Braxton was never again a problem for James. The following day Braxton returned to class as normal and didn't even seem to be aware that there had been a "trial" in his honor. A few days later, however, Braxton would make the unfortunate decision to push a female security officer up against a wall, just for fun.

Nobody was hurt, but the incident was witnessed by two other security officers who were apparently considered more credible witnesses than James and the other four teachers Braxton had threatened previously and whose safety was also apparently considered more important by their fellow police officers—because from that day forward, Braxton was removed from Earl Warren and was never seen nor heard from again.

James bought a round of drinks to celebrate at the Starving Writer and found that in the post-Braxton era he was able to relax just a little in his difficult morning class. But he also wondered, *what would happen to Braxton Young?* Yes, James's problem had been solved—and he couldn't help but be happy that Braxton was gone from his life. But Braxton was going to be a problem for another school and another teacher once his suspension was up. And after Braxton finally dropped out of high school, what exactly would the future of a kid like that be?

CHAPTER 18

ILLITERACY AND "WILDLIFE"

As an inexperienced teacher, James didn't fully appreciate the difference between high-stakes and low-stakes writing assignments—both for the class and, more subtly, for himself and how he perceived student progress.

This became an issue in his problem morning class, as most of the work James had assigned was work-sheet oriented—low-stakes assignments that the better students completed with ease and the rest of the class either partially completed or derisively turned in with only their doodles for a zero.

The assignments were so basic—and so numerous—that James hadn't paid as close attention to them as he would a take-home paper or an exam. He assumed that students not turning in these assignments were simply not trying—and he hadn't considered the possibility that there were students in the class who weren't turning in the work sheets because they were so behind academically that they weren't capable of understanding them—as was the case with Tashecka Mills.

James made this horrifying discovery during an in-class essay exam he decided to give to his very unhappy morning class, mainly because so few of them would take a homework assignment seriously. The exam was a simple one, based on the short story "Arnie's Test Day" that his friend

Robert Sullivan had used so effectively during the summer. James had his students argue, in a five-paragraph essay, whether they agreed or disagreed with Arnie's decision to cheat on his exams.

He had designed the assignment to essentially walk his students through the process of writing the essay by providing a template they could simply fill in, rather than having them write an essay completely from scratch, which the majority of his students were incapable of doing.

James considered the test to be so easy he almost felt guilty assigning it. Keisha's reaction to the assignment, which she considered far too difficult and time consuming to be bothered with during class—in her mind a social occasion—was predictable.

"You be buggin', mister!"

Nevertheless, this was an exam, and even Keisha Sanders felt an obligation to try, as did the rest of the class—except for Tashecka Mills. Tashecka stared blankly ahead, not even looking at the story or the provided work sheet. James went over to help.

"I didn't really understand the story, mister," Tashecka said as she continued to stare into space.

James assumed Tashecka simply hadn't read the story, which was very short and easy to understand. Nevertheless, he offered to sit down with Tashecka to help her get started.

"Do you understand the instructions, Tashecka?"

"Not really, mister."

"Okay. I want you to read the story and write an essay either agreeing or disagreeing with Arnie's decision to cheat on his exams."

Tashecka's blank stare told James he hadn't gotten through to her. He tried again.

"Why don't you just tell me what you think? Should Arnie have cheated or not?"

"Who Arnie?" Tashecka asked as she turned to look at James.

"Did you read the story, Tashecka?"

"No."

"Why don't you read it now?"

"I don't read so good, mister."

Normally James would have thought Tashecka was just fooling around—"playing him" as it were—but there was an earnestness in Tashecka's answer that gave James pause.

"Why don't you read a little of it to me, and we can talk about it," James tried.

Tashecka's brow furrowed as she struggled to read the title: "Arn-i-es t-est day."

Tashecka was fourteen and could barely read.

James was stunned, but he had her continue with the first line of the story anyway so he could get a better idea of how bad the problem was. Tashecka stumbled through the first sentence, taking about a minute to do so while mispronouncing virtually every word. After she was done, James asked if she could summarize the sentence.

"I don't even know what I just read, mister."

James had Tashecka skip the story and instead simply write a paper on what she thought of cheating. The "paper," which consisted of one largely incomprehensible paragraph written in a six-year-old's scrawl, was at about the same level of her reading, James guessed.

James dutifully took his concerns to Kevin, but after some inquiry, was told there was really nothing the school could do as Tashecka's parents were adamantly against special education classes for their daughter. James was frustrated. How could a student like Tashecka have advanced to the ninth grade?

"She's not even close to the worst I've seen," Kevin mumbled as he glanced over Tashecka's scribbled paragraph and handed it back to James.

Leslie would later explain to James that there was an honest debate as to whether students like Tashecka should be mainstreamed or put into special education classes and that there were good arguments on both sides.

Special education teachers often had specialized training and could work with those students on a more individual basis. On the other hand, the stigma of being put in a special education class might outweigh the benefits for many students.

Leslie's best advice was to find some materials that Tashecka could work with so she could at least be functionally literate—and that, luckily for James, she had some books at home that she would bring in for him to use.

Over the next several weeks, James used Leslie's materials with Tashecka with some success. To his surprise, Tashecka actually displayed a degree of enthusiasm when presented with work she could understand. Even more surprising to James was Keisha's response. Although Keisha wasn't overtly supportive, she did leave Tashecka alone to do her work, perhaps understanding on some level that her friend really needed the help.

It was at about this time that the "wildlife" began to appear at Earl Warren High School.

The "wildlife" problem at Earl Warren wasn't something James had been aware of, but wildlife apparently existed in abundance at the school—hiding behind the walls and underneath the floors, in the furniture, and all the cracks and crevices of the concrete building the whole time, patiently observing James's classes and figuring out the best time to strike. And when the wildlife did decide to come out of their hiding places within the deep recesses of Earl Warren High School, all hell broke loose.

In retrospect, James should only have been surprised the wildlife hadn't surfaced earlier. Earl Warren High School, like most other public school buildings James had visited, wasn't exactly immaculate. There was always the faint stench of urine near the bathrooms, which was often not so faint, and spillages of one kind or another in the classrooms or in the hallways would often go unattended for hours.

And although trash was collected regularly, not all of it actually was.

There was always some litter that got left behind in the classrooms and in the hallways—and when it did, nobody seemed to take responsibility for it. Indeed, certain pieces of rubbish seemed to take on a kind of permanent residency at Earl Warren that would become as familiar to the careful observer as any of the school's students or staff members. In short, it was the type of place where the janitorial staff would eventually get around to doing whatever it was they were supposed to do—where "eventually" might be a while.

James would probably not have even noticed his first wildlife encounter at Earl Warren if it weren't for Danielle Williams's horrified expression just as class was getting started one Thursday afternoon as she pointed with a trembling finger at the fearsome creature which stood on its hind legs atop James's desk, trying to figure out how it was going to steal James's apple.

James almost laughed out loud after the initial shock of seeing the little gray mouse, who seemed to be under the impression that it could somehow abscond with a piece of fruit that outweighed it by at least sevenfold—and pull off this caper in front of an entire classroom full of human witnesses.

Someone screamed.

The scream, however, was not directed at the mouse atop James's desk, which by then had realized it wasn't getting the apple and had scampered into an open drawer, deep into the recesses of the furniture and out of sight, but to a small packet of James's almonds that were scuttling across the floor—the stolen booty of another emboldened city mouse.

James nearly exclaimed, "It's got my nuts!" but caught himself just in time to save his reputation.

Instead, he quietly watched his nuts disappear underneath a bookcase at the back of the room amidst the screams of every student in the class who were now standing on their chairs in a panic. Although James's students endured all sorts of real, sometimes life-threatening dangers in their lives and would often boast of their fearlessness in the face of bullies and gangsters, the sight of a harmless little mouse at school terrified them all somehow—the macho along with the meek.

Over the next week, things got far worse.

When the administration got wind of the numerous mouse sightings—now happening with regularity throughout the school—they responded, as they often did, by over responding. Whatever extermination techniques the school employed did seem to work on the mice, but they also succeeded in bringing far more repulsive creatures out from behind the walls—the giant flying cockroaches.

James had a particular revulsion toward the New York City variety of giant flying cockroaches as they were huge, fast, and most disgustingly, flew in an unpredictable manner, sounding like a miniature helicopter and weren't shy about landing on a person.

Actually, James had a near phobia to this variety of cockroach as a very large one had landed in his hair as a small child, causing him no small amount of distress at the time. So when the giant flying roaches showed up in large numbers one Monday, James nearly lost his mind.

The plague of giant flying cockroaches lasted for about a week. As James understood the situation, the entire school had been bombed with insecticide over the preceding weekend, and the roaches that were repulsing everyone, driven out of the walls by the poison, were actually in the process of dying.

This information did not comfort James, who was expected to remain calm and professional whenever one of the Buick-sized beetles was seen crawling across the blackboard or flying across the room—and then be brave enough to dispatch the winged vermin as necessary.

It was a week of hell for James. But all James's problems were put into sobering perspective soon after the wildlife problem finally subsided at Earl Warren.

James had been watching the evening news the night before with Sue when the shootings in the Bronx near Gun Hill Road were reported. It was drug-related gang violence—and even though there were fatalities, it wasn't considered important enough by the local station to be the top story.

"Don't some of your kids live around there?" Sue looked questioningly at James.

The reality that many of his students lived in such dangerous parts of the city suddenly hit James. As a native New Yorker, he had seen many of its bad neighborhoods—but usually from the safety of a car or a subway train and always during the daytime.

His kids had to spend their lives in those neighborhoods—areas of the city where multiple shootings sometimes weren't considered important enough to be the lead story on the local news.

James hoped they all were all right.

The next day, James noticed Alphonse Martinez, a nice kid and a reasonably good student in his midmorning class sitting in the back—quiet and inattentive. And as the class came to an end, James could see that Alphonse was crying. James went over to see if he could help.

"I'm sorry, mister. My best friend got shot last night. He died."

What do you say to a fourteen-year-old boy whose best friend was just shot to death? Alphonse's friend, a kid who was just in the wrong place at the wrong time, added one more person to the horrible statistic of young people killed because of drug-related violence in the inner city. And the greater tragedy was that Alphonse Martinez would not be the last student James would have at Earl Warren whose life would be forever changed because of the deadly violence related to gangs and drugs.

CHAPTER 19

THE LONG AND WINDING ROAD TOWARD REGENTS EXAMS AND SUMMER BREAK

As the school year labored on through the winter holidays and spring break and onward toward the finish line that was the summer, the reality of what they had gotten themselves into began to take its toll on the teaching fellows.

James had been lucky in that most of the faculty and administration at Earl Warren had been dedicated to their mission of turning the school around—and many of them, like Leslie Brooks and Catherine Angel, were also very talented teachers who had taught him a lot over the course of the year.

He was also lucky that he had found Leslie to be his friend and mentor and was fortunate that the pettiness that ended Robert Sullivan's career in the New York City public school system hadn't sabotaged his—even if he had the audacity to break a few rules like making sure his kids weren't hungry at the end of the day and throwing Jimmy Wiggins a birthday party.

Others were not so lucky.

Without good mentors or caring administrations to support them, many of the teaching fellows decided to drop out of the program at the end of their first year. Some dropped out just because they'd had enough. A few, like Robert Sullivan, were forced out because they didn't get along with their superiors.

Closest to James at Earl Warren was his friend Jane Sherwin, who never quite clicked with any of her students and knew within the first couple of months that she wasn't meant to be a teacher. Jane decided to call it quits at the end of the year and accepted a position in the private sector but at a firm in Austin, Texas, instead of her hometown of New York City where she hoped her work life would be a little more laid-back and her home life would be a lot less expensive—and with the comforts of a house to replace her cramped apartment and a car she could swap for her hated commute on the crowded subway.

Kevin was originally unhappy at the prospect of trying to fill the vacancy, but a prospective graduate of Columbia University's Teachers College who also had a BA in English from Harvard was interested in the position, as he was looking to teach at a high school like Earl Warren so he could "give something back."

"Teachers College and Harvard!" Kevin repeated with a giddy expression and a bounce in his step the entire afternoon after his interview with a guy by the name of David Greene. James hoped David would live up to his impressive paper credentials in the classroom when he started in the fall. But James's personal experience had severely tempered his expectations for someone like David Greene—academically talented but untested in the classroom—from what they might have been a year prior.

Jane Sherwin wasn't the only teaching fellow having second thoughts about staying. Andy Stein had confided to James that although he would probably finish the program, he would try to find work in a better public school or a private school once it was over—and maybe try to write a book.

Jan Walker seemed to be doing all right—although James had heard from some of his students that she wasn't the greatest teacher in the world. But Jan was young and had both the energy and the temperament to deal with all the behavioral issues, which vastly increased the odds of her staying at Earl Warren for a while.

James had heard similar stories from the other members of his cohort at Benjamin Harrison and Taft and wondered how many of them would be teaching at their assigned schools two years into the future.

He had heard that Lauren Weiler had been completely overwhelmed with behavioral problems in her progressively designed classes the first week of the semester and that she had quickly done an about-face and turned into something of a strict disciplinarian—taking Joseph Biles's advice to heart, it seemed.

James had also heard that Lauren and her faithful debate partner Gerald Houston had become an item and had taken their debate sessions to a new level, James imagined.

As for James, he felt much of the same conflict as when he left the legal profession. He was generally succeeding as a teacher, and he still believed he was doing some good in the world, although in a much smaller way than he had originally hoped.

But the daily grind of the teaching profession—dealing with the many diverse problems of his students that often went well beyond academics and that James was often powerless to do anything about, the challenges of maintaining a degree of creativity and spark in his classes as well as order, and negotiating the many senseless rules and regulations of Earl Warren and the system generally—was beginning to wear James down.

And although he believed in the mission of the Teaching Fellows program, he was beginning to understand that unless things changed drastically over the next year or two, he would be one of the many in the program who would continue their teaching careers elsewhere if he elected to remain in the profession—leaving their assigned "at need" schools for greener pastures.

Indeed, James found himself thinking about his career and his future more and more as the school year began to mercifully wind down. And as the summer grew closer and the days grew warmer, classes became less productive as students and teachers alike lost focus on school as they looked forward to their long summer break.

For students, however, there was also the pressure of the upcoming Regents exams, which would be proctored—and then graded—by the Earl Warren faculty.

James was surprised that there wasn't a rule prohibiting a school from grading its own Regents exams—particularly the English Regents as the essay portions of the exam were subjective and could be graded more leniently by sympathetic or self-interested teachers, resulting in grade inflation. The many conflicts of interest were obvious—especially at a failing school like Earl Warren where jobs were on the line if too many students failed—yet the practice was, apparently, commonplace.

Kevin's interpretation of the grading instructions for the English Regents essays only confirmed James's fears. Although standardized grading rubrics were provided, the interpretation of those standards was, like any set of rules, subject to interpretation—and Kevin's very loose and creative reading of the grading guidelines suggested to James that Kevin would have made a very decent lawyer had he chosen to go that way.

Kevin ended his talk with the faculty with his usual disclaimer when it came to grading. "But I can't actually tell you what to do."

The Regents grading itself proved to be a fun and relaxing break for the faculty. Students had a few days off during the process, and the empty hallways of Earl Warren were a welcome contrast to the chaos that normally graced them.

The English department faculty gathered in the school library for their grading sessions. Kevin provided some school-sponsored coffee and donuts for breakfast, and the faculty brought in additional supplies— some homemade and some store bought—to fuel the grading through the remainder of the day.

The procedure for grading the Regents essays was to grade them in pairs. Both teachers had to reconcile their grades, and if they couldn't—or if a paper received a failing grade—a third teacher would be required to review the work. Although this procedure seemed reasonable to James, in practice Kevin's instructions to the faculty, combined with their general sympathy for their own students, resulted in very few failing papers.

The atmosphere was jovial, with faculty reading the most egregiously nonsensical answers aloud for everyone's amusement. And if an objective standard were being applied, less than a third of the papers James graded should have passed. Yet few essays actually failed.

Either there was a liberal interpretation of the rules as provided by Kevin, or in some cases, teachers had sympathy for students they liked and gave them credit for "trying really hard," giving them the benefit of the doubt even though those students should not have passed based on merit alone.

And James wondered—as the grading came to a close and he looked at the very small pile of failing Regents exams—was this cheating?

Every liberty had been taken to inflate students' scores short of passing everyone who showed up. Yet he didn't think Leslie and Catherine and many of the other teachers would think what they were doing was wrong. In their minds, they were helping out students they knew were trying but just weren't as prepared as they should have been.

But was this really helping them? Didn't schools have the difficult and thankless task—indeed, the obligation—to evaluate their students honestly?

What would happen to those students if they ever gave college a try? How would they feel when they discovered that they couldn't pass a remedial English class at a community college after being certified as academically competent with a Regents diploma by the State of New York?

Yes, one could make the case that the policy of allowing Earl Warren to grade the English Regents exams of its own students might technically not have been cheating. But one could also make the case that the inflated pass rate this policy produced was just one more way students had been cheated by the New York City public school system.

CHAPTER 20

SUMMERS OFF: OR HOW JAMES LEARNED TO STOP WORRYING AND LOVE THE BOARD OF ED.

The culmination of the school year for the remaining members of the senior class was graduation and the handing out of diplomas—but for teachers, it was a short visit to the bursar's office and the handing out of a small stack of paychecks that would finance their two-months-long summer vacations.

James had, at the beginning of the school year, viewed taking the entire summer off as a wasteful perk and had even considered teaching summer school at the time. This was because James had been conditioned from an early age to be something of a workaholic—a trait law school and his legal career would only reinforce.

Indeed, before his marriage to Sue, James often found himself embracing the challenges of his former profession, taking pride in the insane number of hours he put in at the firm and actually looking down on people who worked normal hours at normal jobs.

But that was then.

Now all James could think about was running away for a while. Leslie had been right again—summer vacation was one of the greatest perks of the teaching profession, and James would have had to have been in very desperate need of money to teach summer school. So James, like every other teacher in the English department, took the entire summer off.

And for a while it was glorious!

James just hung around the apartment for the first couple of weeks, not doing much of anything except sleeping late, swimming in the afternoons, and renting lots of movies to watch because Sue still had to work.

But Sue had arranged to take a very long summer vacation during the least busy time at her not-for-profit environmental organization, which began in late July, and the two spent some of their happiest times together, vacationing around the country without any responsibilities at all.

Well… there was one responsibility. James had to make sure he deposited each of his summer paychecks *after* each of their respective pay dates and not before.

The experience of having nearly absolute freedom was one James hadn't had since at least college but more accurately since childhood during those carefree summers he spent swimming at the beach on Fire Island. And perhaps this was the reason that after around five weeks, his first summer vacation began to weigh on James.

The idea that he was wasting his time and was not being the productive professional he had been brought up to be began to creep into his mind—as did the thought that taking the entire summer off was, in a way, kind of childish.

An invitation from his friend and former mentor Phil Blake to spend the weekend in the Hamptons only made things worse. Sue kept blowing her hair out of her eyes as she silently packed for the trip—always a sign she wasn't pleased about something.

"Do we have to go? All he ever talks about is money, and all she ever talks about is shopping."

"Phil's been a good friend. They have a nice pool, a tennis court… It'll be fun."

James knew Sue hated the Hamptons, preferring the more informal, down-to-earth atmosphere of the Jersey shore or Montauk to the hedged-in mansions of the obscenely successful.

And he knew Sue hated anything to do with his old law firm.

But the truth was that James had kept in touch with Phil more than he had let on—partially because they were friends and partially because Phil was the road back to a career James was, privately, not a hundred percent sure he wanted to leave.

And as James relaxed in a lounge chair on Phil's pool deck, sipping an iced tea on a perfect summer day, James was reminded how much loved the Hamptons. He loved its lavish houses with their heated swimming pools, hot tubs, tennis courts, and multiple-car garages—always filled to capacity with Mercedes and Porches and the like—and a vintage Ferrari, in Phil's case.

And being in the Hamptons reminded James how he had worked his whole life to be in a position to afford such extravagances and how he had, with his change in career, given up his chance of being able to afford anything even close.

Phil rarely made it out to his home in the Hamptons, and his wife, who was used to having the house to herself, often couldn't help but treat Phil as more of a house guest than as her husband. James could also tell that Phil felt uneasy taking so much time off from the firm as he spent half their time together tethered to his Blackberry.

Sue lasted a day.

She made a feeble excuse that she had an emergency at work and took the Jitney back to the city after privately explaining to James that she couldn't take another day of talking to Phil's wife about fashion, her hired help, and what a plastic surgeon could do about her freckles.

"We have absolutely nothing in common. I don't know what you see in those people," Sue angrily whispered to James in their guest bedroom as she hurriedly packed a bag for her trip back to the city.

It was just as well.

Phil had invited James out to the Hamptons, in part because they were friends and in part to try to persuade him to come back to the firm.

As Phil explained as he showed off his beloved Ferrari to James, several of his first-year associates weren't working out as was often the case.

"Spoiled brats. Taking half-hour lunches and feeling entitled to week-long vacations." Phil paused for a moment as he composed his thoughts. "You're one of us. I know you. You want to come back."

James didn't answer, but he knew Phil, the "voice of reason" in his life was right.

"You and Sue... She's a nice girl, but... It's not going to last—no matter what you decide. You're two different people. You want different things out of life."

As the two stood together in Phil's oversized garage, admiring the lines of Phil's Ferrari, James had to admit to himself that he and Sue were, indeed, two very different people. With all the compromises he had made... that Sue had made... could their marriage really work? They needed more time to find out, James decided.

And there was also still a part of James, although a smaller part than a year ago, that felt he needed to do something more meaningful with his life than be a lawyer for corporate America. And despite the many frustrations and setbacks, James did still believe he was doing some good in the world being a teacher at a school like Earl Warren.

Phil's opinion was that James's efforts were going to waste.

"Social Darwinism will work things out as far as the world is concerned. Everybody thinks they're a victim, but people get what they deserve," Phil stated matter-of-factly as he ran a dustcloth over the hood of his Ferrari.

James had to admit that he partially agreed.

He had certainly encountered, in person and on the telephone, his share of irresponsible and sometimes abusive parents whose children seemed destined to follow in their footsteps no matter what he or anybody else did. Keisha Sanders and Braxton Young came to mind.

But he also understood the issue was much less clear-cut than Phil believed it to be.

James had, similarly, met a lot of good kids at Earl Warren—many with responsible, caring parents who happened to be poor for one reason or another—and there were many students who were very smart and willing to work hard to improve their circumstance but who were in constant danger of being overwhelmed by a dysfunctional system and a dysfunctional society. And those kids needed good teachers to help them if they were going to succeed and go to college someday. Perhaps those were the students that fit Leslie's mantra that if you helped just a few of them succeed, it would make your whole career worthwhile.

Phil seemed to understand the situation, giving James another year "in that hellhole they call a school" before he'd see reason and change his mind.

So James turned down Phil's offer.

Indeed, James was even looking forward to starting the new term as exciting changes were happening in the New York City public school system. Michael Bloomberg and Joel Klein, his attorney school chancellor, with all their business savvy were taking over—and they were instituting a new curriculum called Ramp-Up to Literacy, which would standardize much of what teachers did in the classroom. It was a program for which James was scheduled for a special five-day training session along with the other members of the English department.

Surely with more money being spent on classroom training and materials and with such sagacious leadership as Bloomberg and Klein, things would improve in James's second year of teaching at Earl Warren.

CHAPTER 21

YEAR II: RAMP-UP TO LITERACY AND THE BLOOMBERG ADMINISTRATION

James was happy to see all the familiar faces from the English department at the Ramp-Up to Literacy training session that was being held at the end of the summer, not in a public school but in a swank office building in midtown that had upscale, well-equipped conference rooms where the classes would be held.

There were all the usual accoutrements: large, state-of-the-art televisions to display the PowerPoint and video presentations, provided legal pads and pencils, all the coffee and bottled water one could drink, and a very nicely catered lunch for all the participants.

The training would last five days.

At the back of James's mind, there were thoughts of how much this was costing the city, and normally he would have questioned the extravagance of renting such an expensive venue—questioned whether the money was really being spent in the best possible way.

But James wasn't feeling very political that day.

He was feeling, to his surprise, very nostalgic. It had been a while since he had been in a real office building, and he was finding that he missed all the comforts—especially the feeling that he was, again, being treated with the respect he felt a professional like himself deserved.

He even had a fleeting thought about calling Phil and seeing if there was still an opening at the firm and if he could get his old office back.

On one level, it was petty for James to feel this way. He was, after all, only a second-year teacher. But it had been surprising to James just how little respect everyone seemed to have for teachers—veteran teachers and new teachers alike. And it went beyond just students and administrators. There seemed to be little respect for the profession as a whole.

The attitude "those who can, do—those who can't, teach" seemed to permeate the culture to a much greater degree than James was ever aware of before he joined the ranks of the supposedly incapable. And teachers in the public school system were certainly not treated as professionals, often working in horrible conditions and vastly underpaid for the privilege.

Surely good teachers deserved respect.

James had been surprised how much talent it took to be a really good teacher like Leslie or Catherine and how much work it had taken him just to be okay at it. Perhaps the profession's reputation suffered, in part, due to the many bad teachers entrenched in the system, as their sometimes shocking incompetence was more likely to make headlines than the slow and hard-fought progress the many good teachers in the system made, one student at a time.

And perhaps teachers were unfairly blamed for other societal problems affecting their students and their schools that they had no control over. Kevin's mantra—that teachers are blamed for everything whether it's fair or not—came to mind. No wonder so many of them practiced defensive teaching—"covering their asses," as it were.

James wished the system was better—less political—and with the power and, perhaps, also the desire to actually change things. That it could get rid of bad teachers more easily and appropriately reward good ones, find a better way to deal with disruptive students, admit that smaller classes affect student outcomes—especially in schools serving kids from poorer neighborhoods—and spend the money to decrease class size, provide quality preschool education and focus on kids when they were young so they didn't end up academically handicapped like so many of his students at Earl Warren. And most of all, insist on high standards despite all the pressures to dumb them down, with the expectation that its students would attend college, while also providing alternate tracks for students who would benefit more from vocational training. Perhaps the Bloomberg administration would work toward some of these goals, and perhaps this new Ramp-Up curriculum was the start.

Leslie wasn't so optimistic.

"Take what you can from the training. But this Ramp-Up thing is just a fad. The board of ed comes up with mandated teaching methodology all the time. Everyone goes a little crazy for a while, and then we just go back to doing what we were doing before. Most illogical."

Leslie was, however, a little behind the times with her reference to the board of education. Michael Bloomberg had recently changed the name to the Department of Education and made it a mayoral agency. Perhaps things would start to change now that the system was under Mayor Bloomberg's control.

But as James attended the Ramp-Up training classes, he wasn't so sure that Mayor Bloomberg, for all his business savvy—or perhaps because of it—really understood the problems of students like James's or of schools like Earl Warren.

It wasn't that the Ramp-Up program was bad. There were actually some very good suggestions for structuring lesson plans and some interesting ways to do group work. But James couldn't help but notice that the videos and photographs of the classrooms being shown didn't look like his, and that none of the Ramp-Up instructors had ever taught in a New York City public school—let alone one like Earl Warren.

The classrooms pictured were all in new, modern schools with plenty of art supplies, computers, and multimedia centers. And, most strikingly, those classrooms had far fewer children than the thirty-four students that filled James's classes to capacity. The children depicted were also much younger—and mostly Caucasian.

Indeed, the picture being presented was that of a well-to-do suburban middle school whose students came from a very different world than the students at Earl Warren and whose well-appointed modern schools were from an entirely different sphere as well.

One part of the program that showed a complete lack of understanding about the realities of schools like Earl Warren was the requirement of a cross-age-tutoring component, where older students were supposed to read to younger ones to achieve something called "shared motivation." It wasn't that cross-age tutoring was a bad idea—it was probably a good idea in a well-functioning suburban school. But it was a disaster in the making for many of James's students at Earl Warren.

Aside from the harm to many of his kids' self-esteem when they discovered that many elementary-school-aged children were far better readers than they were, some of his students like Tashecka Mills could barely read, let alone tutor anyone. And James had difficulty picturing many of his other students like Keisha Sanders and Braxton Young participating at all—or what it would be like to take a class like theirs on a field trip to a grade school to tutor younger children.

Even Kevin would later admit privately that this part of the program could probably never be implemented in a meaningful way at Earl Warren, saying under his breath, "We'll just have to fake it somehow."

But the aspect of the training that worried James the most—and which caused Catherine Angel no small degree of consternation as well—was the emphasis on group work. It wasn't just that group work would be part of the curriculum. Group work *was* the curriculum. One of the philosophies of this new program was that traditional teaching was somehow inferior because it was teacher centered, while group work was inherently superior because it was student centered.

Whether this was pedagogically sound reasoning was a silly debate in James's opinion. He, the majority of the other teaching fellows, and previous generations of academically talented people had received a top-notch education without ever having done group work. But that was almost beside the point.

Many of James's students simply weren't capable of doing group work effectively. The majority of James's kids lacked motivation and would use the time to socialize, leaving the work to be done by the one student who cared—if the work got done at all.

Even if a teacher could sort through all the friendships and all the rivalries, there were thirty-four kids in a class at Earl Warren, which meant six groups of mostly unmotivated students that would have to be supervised by just one teacher.

It was a logistical nightmare.

The assumption that a more rules-free, student-centered approach was "better" was one that James might have shared with the other teaching fellows in his cohort at the beginning of the program—and a year ago, he probably would have bought into the Ramp-Up to Literacy program quite easily.

But after a year teaching at Earl Warren, James understood that there was no easy answer as to what constituted "better" pedagogy. He had seen Leslie Brooks succeed in a very loosely structured freewheeling class, and he had seen Catherine Angel succeed in a very traditional classroom with strict rules, sitting at her desk the entire period.

Group work was probably great for a small class of highly motivated students and a teacher with the right personality—and completely wrong for a mix that changed any one of those ingredients.

What James had learned from his year of teaching—and one of the few things about the profession he was absolutely certain of—was that good teaching was much more of an art than a science and that good teachers had to adjust their teaching styles to suit their students, their school environments, and their own personalities.

The mandate of using group work—or any other technique exclusively—was doomed to failure. Not because the teaching method itself wasn't valid, but because mandating and standardizing the teaching method handcuffed the good teacher, preventing them from doing their job in the most effective and appropriate manner.

As for the bad teachers—James guessed they would remain bad teachers no matter what method they were told to use.

And this was the real problem with the Ramp-Up program for James and many of the other teachers who cut their summer vacations short to attend the training. It was mandatory. Group work and the Ramp-Up curriculum would now be the required, standard method of teaching at Earl Warren for ninth grade English, and group work would be mandated for most other classes as well.

James felt as if he would have to throw out nearly everything he had learned the previous year and start over again from scratch—with an entirely new method of teaching that he would receive just five days of training to implement and without any real-life, hands-on experience.

This philosophy of standardizing teaching methods came back to the issue of respect for the profession for James. Did the powers that be even think of teachers as professionals? To James, it didn't seem so.

Professionals were respected for their intelligence and expertise—and perhaps most of all, for their ability to use their brains to solve problems—often in creative and original ways. Standardized teaching methods treated teachers like assembly line workers—as if good students were products to be manufactured and teachers could put together a perfect student—if only they all used the same, ideal manufacturing process.

It wasn't surprising that someone from the business world like Michael Bloomberg would see the problem in this way and implement a program like Ramp-Up to Literacy, sincerely believing it to be an improved process that would surely get the products of New York City's public school system—its students—up to spec.

Ramp-Up to Literacy: an easy-to-implement, cost-effective solution.

Years later, James would come across a study out of Johns Hopkins University—Michael Bloomberg's alma mater, ironically—which revealed that none of the many reading programs that claimed to boost student performance, including Ramp-Up to Literacy, could produce meaningful studies that showed strong evidence of effectiveness. Indeed, only a handful could boast proof that they were even moderately effective. Ramp-Up to Literacy, like the majority of the programs looked at, had "no qualifying studies," according to the researchers at Hopkins, to back up its claims of success.

Still, Pearson Education would be awarded a lucrative contract by the city, and Ramp-Up to Literacy would be implemented at Earl Warren.

David Greene, the English department's newest, Harvard and Columbia Teachers College-educated faculty member, nearly scoffed at the concerns of James and the other English department faculty—especially at Catherine Angel's aversion to group work which he felt was "behind the times."

James instantly disliked him.

Like James Hartman of a year ago, David Greene was infatuated with his impressive paper credentials and vastly overestimated his understanding of—and his ability to deal with—the realities of what he had signed up for at Earl Warren.

But unlike James, David just couldn't hack it.

David had a peculiar expression on his face after his disastrous first class of freshman English—as if he just couldn't wrap his head around what had happened to the great David Greene during the past hour of his life.

"They don't appreciate me at all," he said in complete bewilderment as he stumbled into the English office.

James and Leslie exchanged amused glances. Leslie was about to offer some of her usual sagacious advice, when David Greene showed his prestigious degrees to be completely worthless paper and himself to be a complete moron... of the highly educated sort.

"And I had the perfect lesson: a class contract."

David's attitude was that it was his students' fault that they didn't respect or trust him or appreciate "the opportunity he was giving them." He was simply incapable of seeing the world from their point of view, incapable of understanding that he would have to earn their trust and respect, and that his superlative paper credentials—his Ivy League education—meant nothing to them.

So after just two weeks, David Greene quit.

Kevin was beside himself. The school would now have to hire someone to take David's place, and the selection of applicants interested in a position at a school like Earl Warren, now that the school year had started, was rapidly becoming very "bottom of the barrel."

After a week of substitute teachers for David's classes, the school hired a middle-aged guy with a good fifteen years of teaching experience by the name of Damian Poe, who probably got the job because, unlike many of the other candidates who saw no problem arriving at their interviews in jeans and sneakers, Damian appeared outwardly to be relatively normal, dressed rather formally, always in the same tweed jacket and red polka-dotted bow tie.

And he met the requirement of being a certified teacher, although "certifiable" would have been a better adjective to describe Damian Poe—both as a teacher and as a person.

Damian turned out to be a very strange man who, thankfully, mostly kept to himself. And he was a horrible teacher—if one could even call what he did "teaching"—responsible for many of Kevin's ever more frequent migraines, James imagined.

James would occasionally catch Damian leering at female students and not seeming to care that James had noticed. A peek into his classroom would reveal the tweed jacketed, red bow-tied Damian Poe holding a book and reading aloud in a completely inaudible voice while the rest of the class—all thirty-four of his students—wandered about, socializing with each other while completely ignoring Damian's "lesson."

None of Damian's students would study English that year.

There was also one student of James's who wouldn't study English that year—or possibly ever again.

When James read over his class rosters at the beginning of the term, he was happy to see some familiar names back for sophomore English, including Danielle Williams, Gavin Mosely, and Maria Rodriguez in his midmorning class that he had very high hopes for.

But James was horrified to see the duo of Keisha Sanders and Tashecka Mills together again in his morning class—and he wasn't sure he could take another year of the two of them giggling together in the back row at his expense.

James, however, discovered to his great surprise that his fears were misplaced. Keisha and Tashecka barely spoke the entire class on the first day, which to James's great relief, was not in room 237. After class, Tashecka stayed behind and asked James if she could speak to him for a moment.

"Mister Hartman, I need to talk to you. I did somethin' really stupid. I'm pregnant."

"If there's anything you need, just let me know," was the response James's reeling mind was able to produce without missing a beat in a remarkably calm and professional tone, to his mild surprise and great relief.

Tashecka gave James a genuine smile.

"Thank you, mister. I appreciate it."

James was horrified.

It was more than just the sickening fact that a shockingly large number of the fourteen-year-old girls he and his colleagues taught as freshman would come back pregnant as sophomores. It was Tashecka's circumstance in particular—that she was nearly illiterate and soon to be a mother that made James feel queasy.

James had been brought up in a world where his parents and the parents of all his friends and acquaintances were well educated and at least reasonably secure financially. They were all able to pass their education on to their children, not just by making sure they got a good formal education but by educating their children themselves every day in a stable home environment and in numerous ways that couldn't be quantified.

In contrast, Tashecka wouldn't be able to read more than the simplest bedtime stories to her child if she read to her child at all and would struggle, along with her child, with poverty and all the other hardships of being a single mother.

Tashecka would attend another week of classes before disappearing forever from Earl Warren. James would never know what became of Tashecka Mills. He hoped that somehow life would work out for her, but in his heart he knew that Tashecka would almost certainly become part of a grim statistic of young, single mothers—part of a cycle of poverty that was all too common in America.

CHAPTER 22

THE MAGIC OF SHAKESPEARE

James's second year at Earl Warren had a somewhat different complexion than his first, not only because of the new Ramp-Up curriculum and the introduction of mandated group work but also because Kevin had assigned James and the other teaching fellows a wider variety of classes.

Instead of five classes of freshman English, James would now teach two classes of freshman English that incorporated the new Ramp-Up to Literacy curriculum, two classes of sophomore English, which would cover a more traditional curriculum, including one required Shakespeare play and one Regents exam-prep class.

James was not too thrilled about Shakespeare as a choice for the majority of his students who struggled enough with Standard English and whom he felt could connect better with more modern material, preferably written by minority authors. And he wasn't too thrilled about doing a play, as plays were really meant to be seen rather than just read.

But Kevin insisted on at least one Shakespeare play for sophomore English, so James chose the comedy *A Midsummer Night's Dream*, which dealt with the theme of love—something adolescents could easily relate to—and which he hoped would be at least mildly amusing to his class.

As for the Regents exam-prep course, James felt it was a waste of time, but it was something Kevin apparently considered of vital importance—more so to Kevin's career than to the students at Earl Warren, James suspected.

Standardized testing was a large part of the system, and James was again forced to confront the question of whether this reality was something that needed to be changed. James's skepticism of standardized tests began long ago in high school when the SAT scores of his classmates filtered through his grade. Many of the smartest and most creative students at his school hadn't tested so well, while some of the duller tacks in the box had knocked the SAT right out of the park.

And most recently, James had witnessed Martin King thrown out of the New York City public school system on the basis of a nonsensical standardized test—and Martin had been the best teacher in James's entire cohort.

The bottom line for James was that standardized tests assessed mostly the ability to *take* tests—not ability alone. And the proof was that they could be coached. Far from being an equalizer, standardized exams often required serious money for test-prep courses and private tutoring for those who excelled. James wondered how many qualified students without the means to pay for such academic extravagances would take them at all—and even apply to the nation's top colleges and universities.

And because big money was involved in the standardized testing industry, James suspected standardized testing would be difficult to get rid of even if doing so would produce a system that was both better and fairer.

For students like James, the distraction of test prep, although annoying and pointless, wasn't particularly harmful. To students who were struggling to get an education, it was.

James would, in teaching his Regents test-prep classes, devote a lot of valuable time to going over test-taking strategies—time that could have been used to teach his students how to write and how to think.

A lot of valuable time was also being spent by James dealing with the many new challenges created by the recently mandated group work of Ramp-Up. James learned very quickly that he couldn't just randomly assign groups as there were too many social implications—many of which weren't obvious until kids who were rivals of one sort or another would get together in a small group and a fight would suddenly break out.

Even after James sorted out the groups in a way that would avoid social conflict, there was often simply not enough motivation to make the groups work in the way they were supposed to. Either one student would end up doing all the work while the others socialized and end up justifiably pissed off about having to do all the work, or groups without such a leader would only make an effort in short spurts whenever James was close enough to observe. The resulting work, despite James's best efforts, was nearly always substandard.

The main culprit was class size.

There was just no way for James, by himself, to watch thirty-four students split into groups of five or six all at once. Perhaps at a school with more motivated students group work could be successful in such a large class—or, perhaps, the Ramp-Up strategies were designed for smaller classes like the ones pictured in the presentations James saw during his five days of Ramp-Up training.

James would often think back to his small summer class at Benjamin Harrison and how easy it had been to give students the one-on-one attention they needed in that setting. He thought about Javier Ramos and how much help he had been able to give him because the class was so small. Even without his friend Robert Sullivan's help, James figured he would have been able to have had successful group work with a class of twenty or so—even if the group wasn't the most motivated in the world.

Other teachers James would consult on the issue, including Leslie and Catherine, agreed that somewhere around twenty students was an ideal class size, with the ability to effectively manage the classroom deteriorating exponentially with each added student over twenty—particularly in an environment like Earl Warren.

It seemed to James that the system had implemented the Ramp-Up program—a program clearly designed to work with smaller and more enthusiastic classes—without taking the average class size in the New York City public school system into account at all.

Another issue James and the other teaching fellows were having with the Ramp-Up program was the quality of the classroom libraries. Substantively, many of the books were more appropriate for middle school and the reading level of many of James's students. However, nearly all James's students were upset over the reading choices. In addition to students feeling as if they were repeating eighth grade, students constantly complained that there were few title selections that interested them.

The physical quality of the books was another issue that quickly surfaced. It was clear to James that someone had skimped on quality when selling the Ramp-Up libraries to the city for a tidy profit, he imagined. After just the first week, many of the covers were coming off the poorly bound-together pages, and the libraries looked worn and tattered to the great dismay of Kevin, who worried someone important might see them and get the wrong impression of the school.

So after about a month into his second year of teaching at Earl Warren, James felt nearly burned out. Although none of his classes were room 237 horrifying, the lack of flexibility as to what James could do in his classes made it challenging for him to find ways to get his students to do what he considered to be meaningful work.

His midmorning class with Danielle Williams and Gavin Mosely was his best class as he predicted it would be, but Maria Rodriguez—who James had expected to eclipse Danielle Williams as his best student—was, to James's great surprise, having attendance issues.

And when Maria did show up, she was very different from the curious, hardworking teenager he had been so happy to teach freshman year, showing no interest in any of the work she was presented with. She seemed disconnected, sometimes just sitting quietly, staring into space. Sometimes, at James's urging, she would quickly complete whatever assignment was in front of her but without any of the passion or interest she had displayed as a freshman.

James was worried about her.

Telephone calls to Maria's home proved ineffective, as her parents spoke very little English and seemed as confused by their daughter's change in behavior as her teachers. Eventually it was discovered that Maria had become involved with a street gang that apparently didn't value school all that much and that was encouraging Maria to drop out.

James was reminded of the poem "We Real Cool" by Gwendolyn Brooks about a group of kids that drop out of school and live a very fast and very short life—which he presented to Maria on one of the increasingly rare days she would attend school.

"It's about high school dropouts and how their lives come to a tragic end," Maria concluded in a near whisper, eyes averted.

"So why do kids drop out of school so often when it's clearly such a bad choice?" James asked.

"'Cause we too cool for this place, yo!" a student blurted out.

James ignored the comment and the laughter that followed and walked over to Maria's desk.

"Maria, why do kids drop out when they know it's such a bad decision?" James asked Maria directly, trying unsuccessfully to make eye contact.

Maria slowly answered without looking up at James.

"Peer pressure to be cool... Survival... I don't really want to talk about this anymore."

James wanted to do more to help Maria—a child with tremendous potential. But the influence of a street gang in Maria's neighborhood was not something James had any control over—and all he could do was hope that Maria would make the choice to continue her education and somehow resist the enormous pressure to drop out of school.

Needless to say, James was feeling very discouraged and needed something magical to happen to restore his enthusiasm for teaching. And this would come, very unexpectedly, from the Bard himself, William Shakespeare.

As James had feared, *A Midsummer Night's Dream* had not gone over well in his sophomore English classes. Keisha Sanders, upon reading and not understanding the first few lines of the play, threw her book across the room in frustration, cursing angrily and dismissing Shakespeare as "mad wack" and making a similar comment under her breath about James and "White people," which James chose to ignore.

And Keisha was not alone in her dislike for Shakespeare. Even James's best students struggled with the language.

"Why we have to read this, mister?" Danielle Williams demanded after yet another disheartening class.

But James, despite his own misgivings, couldn't really do anything about the curriculum. Kevin had required a Shakespeare play, and there really wasn't any way James could get away with not teaching one. And he felt especially bad for one student in Danielle's class—a very likable young man by the name of Edward Jefferson, who James and some of his other teachers suspected might be mildly retarded.

Unlike Tasheka Mills, a girl with normal intelligence who never learned to read or write past an elementary school level and who probably suffered from numerous undiagnosed learning disabilities that contributed to her functional illiteracy, Edward seemed genuinely slow in every way—to the point that James wondered if he had ever been properly evaluated by any of the schools he had attended.

He thought back to his interview for the Teaching Fellows program with Mrs. Gerwitz and her pointed question about what James would do if he suspected a student in his class was mentally retarded.

And James had done for Edward what he said he would do in that interview.

He gave him special work and extra attention when possible. And James was glad to put in the extra effort for Edward Jefferson, who was a very sweet kid—always friendly and polite and eager to try whatever work James put in front of him. Edward was just really, really... slow.

But Shakespeare was unavoidable, and James spent considerable time thinking about strategies he could use to help Edward understand at least some of the play. But he needn't have worried—because, as James would soon learn, there was a very mysterious and very wonderful magic to Shakespeare.

Edward had been silently—and very intently—reading and rereading *A Midsummer Night's Dream* from the first day James introduced the play. But James assumed he was either just pretending or that he was fascinated with the unfamiliar language somehow. And as the class struggled to understand the basic meaning of the latest stanza James had assigned, Edward slowly nodded his head and grinned.

"Yes. I understand this. I had to read it three times—but I understand this."

James was skeptical as were several in the class who had never seen Edward Jefferson contribute to class discussion and, like James, assumed he was incapable of doing so. But James invited Edward to share his insights anyway.

"Well...," Edward slowly began. "It's like this. It's all about how love is really messed up."

James was both surprised and impressed.

"Yes, Edward, it certainly is. Can you give an example from the play of how love is 'really messed up'?"

Edward slowly nodded as he turned his attention to the text.

"See... this woman Helena, she jealous 'cause even though she as good-looking as this other woman Hermia, this guy Demetrius don't pay no attention to her 'cause he in love with Hermia. I know that 'cause Helena say, '*Through Athens I am thought as fair as she. But what of that? Demetrius thinks not so.*' And then she say, *'Things base and vile, holding no quantity. Love can transpose to form and dignity.*' Here she sayin' that if you in love with someone, you can't really see what's wrong with them. Like my mom, she still in love with my dad even though he drink too much and ain't around no more. And then Helena say, *'Love looks not with the eyes, but with the mind. And therefore is winged Cupid painted blind.*' So she sayin' that when we in love, we blind to how they really is 'cause we ain't lookin' at that person with our eyes no more—and that why Cupid—the little guy with the bow and arrow on Valentine's Day that makes you fall in love— sometimes has a blindfold on."

James stood stupidly at the front of the room with his mouth hang-ing open. Edward looked up from his Shakespeare at James with a big smile on his face.

"It's very beautiful, mister."

"Yes, Edward. Yes it is."

"Wait. He's right?" Danielle exclaimed as she nearly fell out of her seat.

Edward Jefferson would continue to provide wonderful insight into *A Midsummer Night's Dream* over the next several weeks—inspiring the rest of the class to look harder at the play so they too could see the beauty of the text that Edward somehow always saw so plainly.

And despite the considerable amount of thought James's ratio-nal mind gave to figuring out some scientific explanation as to how and why Shakespearean language affected Edward Jefferson the way it did, the best James could ever come up with was that there was, indeed, some sort of very mysterious and very wonderful magic associated with William Shakespeare.

CHAPTER 23

WHEN SMART KIDS DROP OUT

James's concept of a high school dropout was a student with academic deficits or behavioral issues or both—or someone who would leave school early to practice a trade of some sort—or very rarely some genius who would go on to invent the next big thing and change the world.

James fully expected students like Keisha Sanders and Braxton Young to drop out. And many of the students who would drop out of Earl Warren in droves at the age of sixteen certainly fell into James's conception of a typical high school dropout.

What James was unprepared for was that several of his very best students—students with the potential to succeed at good four-year colleges and make something of themselves—would drop out as well, as was the case with his most talented student, and perhaps the most talented student in the entire school, Maria Rodriguez.

James had always wondered how a student like Maria, who had received the highest honors in both grade school and middle school, had ended up at Earl Warren in the first place. Why hadn't she tested for one of the city's specialized high schools—or at least applied to some of the more competitive nonspecialized high schools in the city?

Leslie offered James a blunt explanation over drinks at the Starving Writer—drinks that James, to his great surprise, was beginning to develop a taste for.

"Kids that don't have an effective advocate to negotiate the system get screwed." Leslie took a generous sip of her drink before continuing. "The truth is there aren't very many good high schools in the city. There are the specialized high schools—the ones you're probably familiar with: Stuyvesant, Bronx Science, and so on. They require the SHSAT, which requires good tutoring—and even then you probably won't get in. Then there's the screened high schools. Many of them are quite good, but again, you've got to go through a complicated application process and sometimes an interview." Leslie downed the last of her drink and ordered another. "And then there are the unscreened schools—and a few of them are okay, but most, like Earl Warren, aren't. Our parents didn't help their kids find a good school because they didn't have the ability or the English language skills or the education—or the time because they're working so hard—or sometimes because they just didn't give a shit."

James wondered what the story was with Maria's parents and wondered whether they would even show up to parent-teacher conferences.

James was a lot less stressed out over the prospect of parent-teacher conferences his second year. He knew he would only see a few parents—and mostly the parents of kids he really didn't need to see.

Predictably, Danielle Williams's mom showed up as did Gavin Mosely's. James was happy to have the opportunity to tell them again how much he enjoyed having their kids in his class. Also, predictably, none of James's problem kids' parents showed up—which was a relief in a way but also quite demoralizing.

But as parent-teacher conferences drew to a close, a small, worried-looking couple coyly peeked into James's classroom.

"Mr. Hartman?"

James beckoned the two to come in and take a seat.

"We are Mr. and Mrs. Rodriguez—Maria's parents," Mr. Rodriguez said with a heavy accent as he shook James's hand.

It very quickly became clear to James that the kindly, worried couple that looked up to him with pleading eyes was Maria's biggest obstacle. Although Maria's parents seemed caring and loving, they were, as James would later describe them to Leslie: "lost."

Neither, James surmised, had the capacity to advocate for their child in the complex bureaucracy that was the New York City public school system. And the fact that neither spoke more than a few words of English probably didn't help. James felt powerless as the two expressed complete bewilderment at the changes they were seeing in their daughter as they literally begged James for his help.

Leslie's reaction was unexpectedly cold and unsympathetic. "Looking to you as the authority that's going to solve all their problems. Pathetic." After studying James's shocked reaction, Leslie softened a bit. "Sorry. They cared enough to show up, and it sounds like they couldn't do any better. It just makes me angry—that girl should be getting a full ride to Harvard."

All James could do was promise Maria's parents he would do everything he could—which, in truth, wasn't a whole lot. James was only a teacher—and schoolwork wasn't the problem for Maria, a student who could probably have skipped most of high school and gone straight to college. And Maria was certainly smart enough to understand her choices and their ramifications.

But Maria was also just a kid. And how do you convince a teenager to resist the most intense peer pressure imaginable?

Maria Rodriguez would attend fewer and fewer of James's classes and end up making the unfortunate decision to drop out of school, and all James could do was hope Maria would be able to stay out of serious trouble and somehow get herself back together later in life.

Although peer pressure to drop out of school was often intense, it wasn't the only reason smart kids dropped out. And James would discover, to his great consternation, that Maria Rodriguez wasn't an isolated case. Sometimes the reason smart kids dropped out was because they simply got fed up with all the infuriating frustrations of Earl Warren and with the dysfunctional system itself.

That was the case with Catalina Perez, a junior and a very bright student in James's Regents prep class who had first impressed James by pointing out some subtleties in his favorite poem, Robert Frost's "The Road Not Taken," pointing out that the road less traveled—the less popular paths people sometimes choose to take in life—might not be, as some would romantically like to think, always the best paths for them to take, that the speaker is only speculating as to what he will be saying far into the future about his decision to take the road less traveled by, and that although unusual, sometimes people realize they've made a mistake and go back to that fork in the road to make the other decision later in life.

"Do you think you'll ever go back to being a lawyer, Mr. Hartman?"

Catalina had a way of making James think.

Needless to say, James was astonished to learn that Catalina was in danger of failing out of Earl Warren. Catalina had a genuine interest in literature—one that probably surpassed James's, if truth be told. Under better conditions, James could see Catalina majoring in English and continuing her education to become a professor of the subject. But Catalina's attendance was always spotty—to the point that she was failing all the classes she wasn't interested in, which were all her other classes.

"It's just the whole place—all the rules—the commute… I just can't take it anymore. I mean, I get up at six in the morning to get here early, and there's still a line out the door to go through the metal detectors. And it doesn't matter what I'm wearing—they always go off, and then they search me as if I'm some sort of a criminal. And then I get marked late for class, like it's my fault."

James had often observed long lines just to get into the school, which teachers could happily bypass by entering through a special entrance. To make matters worse, James's students had been complaining of late that one of the scanning machines had been broken for some time and that the process was taking twice as long as usual. And many teachers were, indeed, marking students late who had arrived to school on time but were being held up by a faulty security system.

Broken metal detectors were far from the only problem in a vastly flawed security policy that was time consuming, humiliating, and worst of all, ineffective. James had often wondered why some schools were designated as "scanning schools" and others not. The idea that weapons were more likely to be a problem at Earl Warren than at other city high schools or their suburban counterparts was certainly questionable after incidents like the Columbine High School shootings and other such tragedies in schools across the country.

But the real issue for James was that everyone knew the system simply didn't work.

One of the more uncomfortable conversations James ever had with a student was about the persistence of cell phones in the school, even though such devices were strictly banned to the great protest of both students and parents. Students would either have to pay a rental fee to store their phones, which was a rip-off they could ill afford, or sneak them past security, which was done more often and with relative ease.

"You know how they sneak them in, don't you, mister?" Danielle Williams asked James one day when the issue came up in class.

"I don't think I want to know," was the best answer a blushing James could come up with—to Danielle's great amusement.

James did, indeed, know how cell phones and other contraband were often smuggled into the school—as women often smuggled contraband from one country to another in the most private place possible. The only difference was that border security at an airport could order a strip search while school security guards could not—which was the only part of the security protocol that made sense to James.

When faced with the dilemma of a beeping scanner with no apparent cause, the security guards would eventually relent and let the student pass as they really had no other choice in the matter.

The other way to bypass the metal detectors was to simply bypass the metal detectors—and use a window instead. There were many windows at or near ground level, and none were locked or otherwise guarded. All a student had to do was make arrangements with a friend, and they could get whatever weapons or other contraband they wanted into the school with relative ease.

Whatever method was used, James was made aware of just how ineffective the school's metal detectors were when he learned that a gun had been smuggled into the school one beautiful fall morning.

James had noticed that all the school security guards looked uncharacteristically awake after his first-period class and that there was unusual activity and worried expressions on the faces of the police officers and school administrators surrounding the school security office.

Then he heard the word "gun."

James stopped to listen. Dick Emerson, who had seemingly made the school security office his second home, noticed James and approached him.

"Listen, Hartman. Someone spotted a gun in school. Just keep it to yourself, okay?"

James didn't quite know how to respond—or what to make of the secrecy surrounding the discovery of a firearm at the school. He was a little apprehensive until later in the day when he noted that the security guards had returned to their usual semiconscious selves and that the activity around the security office had subsided.

Nobody was hurt or even threatened by the gun at Earl Warren, but the incident illustrated very clearly for James how ineffective the time-consuming and humiliating security protocol of scanning students actually was.

For a bright person like Catalina Perez who had to deal with being scanned and searched on a daily basis, the security policy at Earl Warren was infuriating as well as insulting. And for Catalina, the hurdle the system had set up just to get into the building of a failing high school, with all its other problems and frustrations once you got inside, was the final straw.

And despite the A James gave Catalina Perez, her spotty attendance notwithstanding, Catalina failed out of Earl Warren.

James would see Catalina in the hallway one last time before she would leave the school forever. She explained how she had not been able to keep up with her other courses and thanked James for the A he had given her, which James assured her she had earned and deserved. As Catalina turned to leave the school for the last time, James felt as if he had to say something more to her.

"Catalina, it's this place. It isn't you. You have a really good mind. Find another way to college. Don't let it go to waste."

James wished he had been able to put his feelings into words more artfully—that he could have said something more brilliant and inspirational to Catalina that would have somehow guaranteed that she continue her education.

Catalina turned back and looked pensively at James.

"Thanks for saying that. I've got a few ideas. I guess I'll have to take the road less traveled, that's all."

With a smile, Catalina Perez turned and headed for the exit—and left Earl Warren forever.

And James was left standing in the middle of the hallway, shaking his head, his lips pursed as another of his smartest kids dropped out under his watch.

CHAPTER 24

THE CHANCELLOR'S VISIT

As James listened to Principal White's voice booming and echoing through the poorly adjusted auditorium sound system, he detected a distinct note of desperation over the slow and methodical monotone that was her usual, sleep-inducing speaking style.

The meeting had been hastily arranged for Friday morning so that preparations could begin that day, but not every faculty member had gotten notification and many were absent. Kevin, however, had made sure the entire English department was present with urgent emails and telephone calls on Thursday evening—and made everyone sign an attendance sheet at the meeting just to be sure everyone had shown up.

The reason for the meeting was that Principal White had been informed that New York City School's chancellor, Joel Klein, was going to visit Earl Warren on the Friday of the following week—so there was little time to prepare.

And although she hadn't exactly said so in her presentation, it was clear to everyone that Earl Warren needed to look like the school it was reputed to be—a school that had turned a corner under Principal White's leadership—and, perhaps more importantly, a school that was properly implementing the Ramp-Up to Literacy program and other changes mandated by Mr. Klein's Department of Education.

"Do you get the feeling her ass is on the line?" Leslie whispered just a little too loudly into James's ear.

James did feel as if Principal White's future was probably on the line—perhaps not from this visit alone but because the school was, despite all the physical renovations and a generally committed faculty and administration, still a mess with many of its larger problems either being ignored or actively denied. And until some of the larger issues, such as overcrowded classrooms and the constant threat of gang-related violence were addressed, James failed to see how tinkering with the curriculum or renovating the facilities would make much of a difference.

Kevin seemed even more nervous at the prospect of Chancellor Klein's visit than Principal White—immediately calling an emergency departmental meeting to make sure Principal White's dictates—and some of his own—were implemented to the letter.

All classrooms used by the English department would undergo a full inspection to make certain they were "print-rich environments" with vocabulary lists, grammar rules, and other appropriate academic decorations plastered over every area of blank wall space.

Kevin had, the night before and with his own money, purchased a large stack of academically oriented posters and diagrams that could be used for this purpose.

The Ramp-Up classroom libraries would be straightened up and re-alphabetized, and the selections that were too obviously falling apart would be removed and stored in the English department office until after the chancellor's visit.

Students using those materials would have to do without them for the week, but this wasn't really a problem because the most important mandate was that student-generated work needed to be prominently displayed, and as there was little student-generated work being produced, Kevin's instruction was to use the class time leading up to the chancellor's visit to generate some.

That meant deviating from whatever lesson plans the faculty had for the upcoming week—Ramp-Up curriculum notwithstanding—and replacing them with something more visually oriented that would look good displayed on a classroom wall, and Kevin suggested everyone purchase colored markers and art paper over the weekend for this purpose.

Kevin would also personally approve every lesson plan being used on the day of the chancellor's visit. All faculty were required to implement group work in accordance with DOE policy, and everyone was reminded to put their names on the board, along with a lesson agenda and a homework assignment. And Kevin reminded everyone, especially Catherine, that faculty were required to stand while delivering their lessons.

"It's not my call. If they see you sitting at your desk or not doing group work, it goes in your file… at the very least."

James looked over at Catherine, who was obviously fuming inside. But it was one thing to assert her rights against Kevin Newcomb and quite another to go up against the chancellor, especially one who had been given more power than any in recent memory and who didn't seem shy about using it.

Catherine kept silent.

The faculty spent a lot of valuable time that Friday and over the next week decorating their classrooms and generating student work for public display. James's students' reaction was that they weren't too thrilled about all the sudden changes to their classroom that greeted them on Monday morning.

"Who comin' ta visit?" was Danielle's cynically delivered question to James as she pretended to admire the new decor.

"And why would you think someone important is coming to visit?" was James's equally sarcastic reply—which garnered him a friendly chuckle from several of the class who were paying attention.

"Because they wouldn't do all this just for us," Danielle answered with a sigh.

James nodded. Danielle was absolutely correct in her assessment—a reality that made James feel both sad and angry, not to mention a little awkward as he was part of the system that was wasting valuable time and energy trying to impress some New York City bigwig.

"There's, like, too much goin' on in here. I can't concentrate, yo!" was Anthony Chavez's take on the newly posted classroom decorations as his eyes darted from wall poster to wall poster.

Anthony was a likable kid but a student who had trouble focusing most days. James suspected that he probably had undiagnosed learning disabilities and was also possibly suffering from attention deficit disorder. But it did seem to James that Anthony was having more difficulty concentrating than usual that Monday morning.

James had recently read some research that countered the widely accepted wisdom—preached loudly by the DOE of late—of making every classroom a "print-rich environment." For many—the learning disabled in particular—such visual assaults of richly printed materials might actually be distracting and detract from learning. James suspected that many of his students probably had undiagnosed learning disabilities, so all the effort he and the others had spent decorating the classrooms had quite possibly done more harm than good.

Perhaps even more frustrating was that, paradoxically, it had been Kevin who had alerted James and the rest of the department to the study. But now that Chancellor Klein was coming to visit, the rooms would be "print rich"—not just because Mr. Klein wanted them that way, but because, James suspected, "print rich" simply looked better, and style over substance was a theme that all too often repeated itself in DOE policy.

Initially James's sophomores took well to the colored markers and large drawing paper they would be using for the next few days to story-board *A Raisin in the Sun*, one of their recent reading assignments. It was a silly lesson, a waste of time with little pedagogical value. And the work produced was mostly quite poor—some of it downright embarrassing to publically post, assuming anyone were to actually look at it closely. James couldn't help but wonder if the cutbacks in art classes in the New York City public school system had contributed to the lack of artistic skill and creativity exhibited by the majority of his students.

One of the few exceptions was Danielle's piece, which not only showed a good interpretation of the material but some decent fine arts skills as well. And Danielle approached the assignment with her usual enthusiasm and energy—until she learned that James intended to post the assignments in the classroom for everyone to see.

"You ain't gonna put it up on the wall, mister. My work is between me and you—and that's it," Danielle stated, her arms crossed as she stood facing James at the front of the classroom.

"Danielle, you do realize yours is the nicest..." James tried.

"That don't matter. I know the only reason we be doin' this is 'cause the chancellor's comin' ta visit and you want some work up on the walls. Mister, if you got any respect for me at all you won't make me put it up."

James felt like a complete hypocrite for even asking, and all he could muster in response was an embarrassed, "Okay."

Danielle looked up questioningly at James.

"Wait. You ain't gonna give me an F are you, mister?"

Danielle was shaking with tears on the rims of her eyes. And James suddenly realized that the distrust students at Earl Warren had for their teachers and the system ran far deeper than he had previously understood.

He wondered what experiences had produced such a degree of distrust and wondered if Danielle Williams—a bright, likable kid with a positive attitude and a strong personality—had been unfairly punished by a past teacher perhaps simply for asserting herself as she was today and, perhaps, when she was completely in the right, as she was today.

"No, of course not. You did a great job on the assignment, so you get an A."

James paused for a minute as he thought of what to say next. An apology seemed in order somehow.

"And if it means anything, I'm sorry I had to give you such a lame assignment."

Danielle smiled faintly.

"I guess the real lesson is that there are some battles you just can't fight. Right, mister?"

James could only manage a slight nod in acknowledgment as Danielle returned to her desk to finish her work.

A few of the other students objected to having their work showcased, but enough of the class didn't seem to care either way and James was able to display some student work as required.

Kevin, of course, wanted more.

"You don't have any graded work you can put up, James?" Kevin asked as he inspected an undecorated area of James's classroom wall.

James actually did have some graded papers he could have displayed, but he had no intention of doing so and less of an intention of sharing that information with Kevin. It took some effort for James to hide his annoyance.

"To be honest, I'd feel very uncomfortable doing that, Kevin. Most students don't want to share their grades—"

"Only put up A work. Then it isn't a problem." Kevin interrupted as he continued his inspection of the classroom.

James probably should have just let it go, but Kevin was suggesting something that was certainly unethical and possibly illegal. And Kevin's attitude was also beginning to piss James off—enough so that he felt it important to respond even if he risked pissing off Kevin in return.

"Well… Actually it is, Kevin. There is a privacy issue here. And I believe it's also a matter of policy…"

"Is that your legal opinion?" Kevin asked sharply, as he turned to face James.

James's objection had clearly succeeded in irritating Kevin, but he couldn't quite tell if Kevin had meant the question to be a cynical or a serious one, so he pretended it was meant as a serious legal query and answered accordingly.

"As an attorney, I have to be careful whenever I express a legal opinion. But off the record, hypothetically... I think a student might have a case if a teacher displayed their graded work without permission."

James never knew whether Kevin took his legal analysis to heart, although he did note that the walls of Kevin's classroom were devoid of graded assignments that Friday morning. None of it mattered though. The chancellor's visit would be canceled—and for the very worst reason imaginable.

On Friday morning, everyone who worked at Earl Warren was on pins and needles awaiting the arrival of the chancellor and his entourage. Every teacher dreaded the prospect of Chancellor Klein and his associates suddenly walking into their classroom and observing them in such an unpredictable teaching environment.

What if a student acted out? What if the lesson plan just didn't work for some random reason? What if the chancellor's expectations were unrealistic for a school like Earl Warren? Would he disapprove of any class in that environment no matter how it went?

First-period classes passed without any sign of Mr. Klein and company, and word got out that the chancellor would be arriving at around eleven thirty for his school tour. And perhaps this was why at around eleven fifteen the proverbial shit hit the fan at Earl Warren really, really hard.

James was walking down a nearly empty hallway on the second floor when it happened. He had just nodded a friendly "hello" to the lone and very bored-looking security guard on the floor when he heard the noise. James didn't immediately understand what the noise was, but the security guard was suddenly very awake and wide-eyed and exclaimed rather loudly, "Oh, shit!" just before running away in the opposite direction.

James, confused, looked toward the strange sound, which was growing louder by the second, but it only dawned on James that he was in trouble after it was almost too late to get out of the way.

The noise that James was hearing—familiar, apparently, to the security guard who had left James standing alone in the middle of the hallway to fend for himself—was the primal yell of several dozen charging teenagers combined with the stampede of their sixty-plus, rubber-soled sneakers squealing on the linoleum floor as they rounded the corner in what seemed like one large chaotic mass—heading straight for James.

James ran.

His first instinct was to head for the stairs and get out of the building somehow—but to his horror another group, at least as large as the first one, burst through the stairwell doors at the other end of the hallway, charging toward James from the opposite direction. James's only option was a classroom in the middle of the hallway, which he prayed would be unlocked.

He tried the door.

There was some resistance, but the door finally opened and James quickly dove inside—greeted by several horrified screams which he quickly realized were from two very frightened students hiding inside who had been trying to hold the door closed.

James kept low, his body braced against the door as anarchy ruled in the hallway on the other side. There was much screaming and yelling and objects being thrown—and there was something over the intercom from Principal White about the school being on lockdown in her usual expressionless monotone… and to remain calm.

There was an occasional attempt from the outside to open the classroom door—but James was firmly pressed against it now—and it would have taken a serious effort to dislodge him, which, fortunately, never happened. James looked over at the two students who had taken refuge with him—obviously terrified. James wanted to reassure them, but as he was fairly terrified himself, he remained silent, realizing all too well that he wasn't in a position to reassure anybody.

The police sent a small army into Earl Warren to secure the school and restore order within ten minutes or so. They made a number of arrests—but like the incident James witnessed on the subway, the vast majority of the rioters would never face any consequences for shutting the school down for the day or for the large amount of property damage they had caused.

Fortunately, there weren't any serious injuries. But the incident illustrated just how out of control Earl Warren really was—that order at the school was upheld by the thinnest of threads and could be lost at frightening speed and without warning. And it caused James to seriously consider, for the first time, whether he really wanted to continue teaching in such an environment and whether all the efforts being made on the school's behalf were really all in vain.

As for Chancellor Klein, he was forced to cancel his tour—and he never rescheduled.

The cause of the riot was never made clear, and although there were rumors it was intended to coincide with the chancellor's visit, officially it was dismissed as just a bad coincidence.

James was nearly certain it had been planned.

Perhaps it had been conceived as simply a joke in the minds of the students who participated—the chancellor was coming to visit, and to their teenage sensibilities, it would be really funny to destroy their school that day.

But James suspected there was more to it than that.

Perhaps the riot was a protest of sorts—a protest against a week of being ignored by the faculty and administration who were too busy putting on a show for their chancellor, Joel Klein; a protest against dressing up the school in the phony garb of bogus student work and meaningless "print rich" décor, much of which now littered the floors of the classrooms and hallways—ripped down from the walls and destroyed by the angry mob.

CHAPTER 25

REASSESSMENT

The school wasn't ever quite the same after the riot canceled the chancellor's visit—and neither was James.

The mess was cleaned up eventually, and "more or less" as was the usual practice with the janitorial staff, but there was a subtle difference in the way everyone related toward one another. Security was beefed up somewhat, although the additional show of force seemed counterproductive somehow, and James failed to see how the school could prevent another uprising if the students ever decided to organize one—something that didn't seem likely, given the even lower amount of interest the students seemed to have for anything related to school after the incident.

It was a lack of enthusiasm James found that he shared—and suspected many of the other faculty and administration shared as well.

For James, the year slowly dragged on—forever, it often seemed—until springtime when the Regents exams finally came around again and gave the faculty a much-needed break from the slog everyone just wanted to be done with so they could collect their stack of paychecks and disappear for the summer.

Year two hadn't been a disaster for James, but it had worn him down severely.

Long gone was his youthful idealism—his dreams of having a real impact on his school and, perhaps, even on the system itself. Gone also was his enthusiasm for teaching, and perhaps most importantly, the energy that James had in abundance at the beginning of the Teaching Fellows program. He understood now that he and the others in the program would have only a negligible influence on their schools and on the system—if any at all.

James hoped that his efforts had helped point a few of his students in the right direction.

And in a small way, they had.

He had helped Danielle Williams and Gavin Mosely clean up their writing and develop critical thinking skills in a way they might not have if they had found themselves in a class with a poor English teacher their first two years in high school. And although both would soon forget the classes they had with the tall guy in the khaki pants, dress shirt, and tie—that teacher they had for two classes of English—Mister Hartman—during their freshman and sophomore years at Earl Warren High School, his efforts did end up helping them both—if only just a little.

Gavin Mosely and Danielle Williams would both attend City College, and both would be prepared enough to pass their introductory writing classes. Gavin would struggle a bit academically but would eventually graduate and end up having a career as a financial aid specialist at the college.

Danielle would, after a challenging first year, hit her stride and graduate with honors, making her mother very proud to see the first in their family graduate from college. And Danielle would go on to nursing school to pursue her dream of having a career in the medical profession.

Both would live happy and full lives.

But at the time, James couldn't know this and he suspected that most of his energies were being wasted—and this knowledge discouraged him greatly. Successful teachers like Leslie and Catherine had grown to accept this reality—that their job, the way the system was set up, was to work very hard help improve a few lives in a small way. And accepting this had helped them maintain their enthusiasm throughout their careers in spite of the system and in spite of the daunting realities many of their kids faced outside of the system—and in spite of the painful reality that much of their hard work would be for nothing.

But Leslie and Catherine were exceptional teachers who loved what they did—and more the exception than the rule, James observed. Many more of James's tenured colleagues—although competent enough—were burned out and just hanging around to reach whatever total accumulation of years in the system they needed to maximize their pension benefits.

Norman Griffin was a good example.

Norman wasn't a bad teacher, but his heart was clearly elsewhere—probably back in the 1970s where he had the best times of his life, from what he could remember of them, during his brief career as a bassist touring in a rock 'n' roll band that often opened for some famous acts back in the day.

Apart from some wild stories of life on the road living a rock 'n' roll fantasy, Norman had often confided in James that he would have quit teaching in the public school system a long time ago if it hadn't been for the way the pension system was set up. Norman had twenty-four years' credit. Just another six years and he would hit the magic milestone of thirty years—and then he could retire with full benefits.

"Just another six years. Just another six years." That was Norman's mantra of late.

James couldn't imagine spending so many years working for the Department of Education or wandering the halls of a school like Earl Warren, counting down the years to a full pension. And increasingly, as he graded Regents exams with Leslie—forced to give passing grades to many more kids than deserved them under Kevin's lax interpretation of the grading rubrics—James knew that if he stayed another year at Earl Warren, it would likely be his last.

Increasingly he was also becoming frustrated with the teaching profession itself—an issue he and Sue would often argue about.

"There are other public schools and lots of private schools you would be happy in," Sue repeatedly reminded James.

But James wasn't so sure that he wanted to spend the rest of his life as a teacher—even at a better school.

To that end, he would visit his friend Phil Blake in the Hamptons alone that summer while Sue took some time off to visit her parents in Idaho. And although there wasn't a position at the firm immediately available, Phil was reasonably sure that one of his new hires wouldn't work out by the following summer—as was often the case. And James understood, as he tried to prepare himself for another difficult year at Earl Warren, that he would have to make some very important and very hard decisions over the next year—both professionally and personally.

CHAPTER 26

YEAR THREE: OVERCROWDING, REGENTS PREP, AND THINGS GET ORWELLIAN

James first thought it was his imagination that Earl Warren was even more overcrowded and disorderly than usual on the first day of school of his third year. There was always chaos in the hallways, but that first day he could barely make his way through the throngs of teenagers on the way to his morning classroom.

When he arrived at his first class of the new semester, James was disheartened to see that his mind hadn't been playing tricks on him and that the school was, indeed, filled beyond capacity.

The maximum class size in New York City public high schools was supposed to be thirty-four—which was far too large to teach a class like English effectively in James's opinion and in the opinion of Leslie, Catherine, and every other veteran teacher James had talked to about class size.

This was true, especially for the population of students at Earl Warren, who mostly lacked motivation, were often behind academically, and who needed lots of individual attention if they were going to succeed. James's first-period class exceeded the already bloated legal maximum by two.

His last class of the day would exceed that stated maximum by six, for a total of forty.

As James took attendance in that last-period class, his overflow students sitting on windowsills and standing for lack of seats, he was nearly overcome by sheer frustration. How was he expected to accomplish the almost impossible task of teaching this class effectively, using the mandatory teaching method of group work no less, when there wasn't even enough space in the classroom to fit all the students the system had dumped into it?

Forty students in a non-lecture class was absurd. And for a school like Earl Warren, the norm of thirty-four students in a class was also absurd. If there was one thing James was absolutely sure would improve the chances of success for students at Earl Warren, it was reducing class size—an issue that the people in power always seemed to skirt around or outright deny as having anything to do with student outcomes.

But if that were the case—if it were really true that class size didn't matter—why were all of James's classes at his fancy private high school capped at eighteen students, with some seminars having as few as six?

There always seemed to be money for new computers and art supplies in the public school system—and in the case of Earl Warren, money for a complete renovation of the building. But there never seemed to be any money to fix the one problem that could actually solve a lot of problems— making classes significantly smaller so it would be possible for teachers to give students, especially at-risk students, the attention they so desperately needed.

James couldn't help wondering if the system had, in cramming so many students into Earl Warren in his third year, signaled that it had given up on the school. There had really never been a complete recovery from last year's riot on the day Chancellor Klein was supposed to visit, and perhaps such a decision had been made somewhere in the upper recesses of the DOE bureaucracy.

Or, perhaps, the DOE was just being its usual clueless self.

Either way, there wasn't any immediate solution anyone could offer to James or the many other teachers dealing with overcrowded classrooms that term. School administration would give vague promises that the problem would be dealt with, and the UFT representative at Earl Warren just shrugged his shoulders when James asked him if there was anything he could do about the situation.

And there were other signs that Earl Warren was now out of favor with the DOE.

There seemed to be an even greater emphasis on Regents prep than usual, and Kevin was far more stressed out about the importance of the percentage of Earl Warren students passing the Regents exam than in past years, assigning James three Regents prep classes in addition to his over-crowded class of sophomores and a class of seniors.

Kevin reasoned that James had taken more standardized tests than anyone else in the department—including the bar exam—and was, there-fore, the best choice to teach the all-important Regents test-prep classes.

James, for his part, was too tired to argue with him.

In truth, although he considered test prep to be a waste of time and possibly even detrimental to an academically struggling student popula-tion, he was secretly happy to have an easy schedule of classes he mostly wouldn't have to think about. But as he looked over his class rosters, James was also saddened to see that there would be no more classes with Danielle Williams or Gavin Mosely. And when James stood in front of his classes on the first day, he found himself looking for the pair in their usual seats together in the front row, lamenting that he wouldn't hear of their adven-tures during summer break or have the opportunity to watch either of them grow further in their academic and personal lives.

But James was also quite relieved not to see Keisha Sanders's name on any of his rosters. He wondered briefly if she had finally dropped out but later discovered she was still at Earl Warren and as obnoxious as ever. But whatever the reason for Keisha's absence, James was quite happy that day not to be one of the unfortunate teachers assigned to deal with Keisha's antics for a change.

The other bright spot for James was that Kevin had, in exchange for giving James so many Regents prep courses, given him a class of seniors that James would have great flexibility with. James decided, against Kevin's advice, to have them read George Orwell's *1984*, a novel James considered to be one of the most important ever written for its warning against powerful, totalitarian government that controls its population by using surveillance, propaganda, and by keeping most people poor and ignorant.

To his surprise, both Leslie and Catherine agreed that teaching *1984* was a bad idea.

"They hate that book, like Klingons hate tribbles," Leslie stated, raising one eyebrow in a Mr. Spock-like fashion.

Catherine agreed wholeheartedly—minus the *Star Trek* reference—and James couldn't convince anyone who would listen to his grand plans for *1984* otherwise.

It was one of the few times James would ignore Leslie's advice.

He reasoned that his passion for the book and his legal take on privacy issues and limiting government power combined with his ability to relate the book to current events would make his class on *1984* different.

He was wrong.

Not only did the class intensely dislike the novel, they displayed a shocking lack of interest—which in some cases was seemed more like a purposeful dislike—of news, government, or any of the big human rights issues in Orwell's novel despite all of James's efforts to bring in related newspaper articles of current events and real-life legal cases to supplement the book.

It was almost as if his class had somehow been conditioned not to want to look at these sorts of important issues that affected their lives—conditioned not to follow the news or be interested in politics and government and ultimately conditioned not to register to vote in large numbers.

James was reminded of the section in *1984* where the population was forced, in a ritual called the Two Minutes of Hate, to watch a film of Emmanuel Goldstein, a purported terrorist who advocated such values as freedom of speech, freedom of the press, freedom of assembly, and freedom of thought—and taught to hate all those freedoms while learning to love their oppressor, Big Brother.

It was, however, a response to the pyramidal structuring of Orwell's dystopian society that really caught James's attention. James had asked Sophia Gomez, a good student—but who, like the rest of the class, hated *1984*—about the different groups that made up society in the novel: the Inner Party, the Outer Party, and the Proles.

Sophia explained, correctly, that the Inner Party was tiny but had all the power, that the Outer Party represented a small, fearful, and powerless middle class, and that the Proles were everybody else who were kept poor and uneducated.

"The people in charge don't even consider the Proles to be human beings, 'cause they say that 'Proles and animals are free.' So it's almost better to be a Prole than in the Outer Party, 'cause at least we free."

Although Sophia hadn't realized what she had said, James immediately picked up her use of the word "we" to describe the Proles—the poor, uneducated, and largely ignored majority of George Orwell's dystopian society that the ruling class considered to be on the same level as animals.

"We."

His first class of freshman English had told him as much two years prior—that the system had put them at Earl Warren because it had decided they weren't going anywhere in life and that, at some level, his students understood that they had been designated by those in power as the underclass.

And as James struggled with his overcrowded classes in his now seemingly discounted school and tried his best to cope with all the other issues his kids had to deal with in their often ignored, crime-ridden neighborhoods, he thought about the structure of American society generally, and he couldn't help wondering if the powers that be subscribed, if only just a little, to the slogans of the ruling party in George Orwell's *1984*: "War is Peace, Freedom is Slavery, and Ignorance is Strength."

CHAPTER 27

TENURE AND THE GAME OF TAG

Fall turned into winter, which seemed to last forever before finally turning into spring.

James barely noticed.

He had spent all his remaining enthusiasm teaching *1984*, and the only thing he had to show for it was that his class was noticeably happier after they had moved on to less interesting material.

"If you're going to apply to a different school, you should probably start looking pretty soon, don't you think?" Sue asked James for the third time one evening as she sat at the kitchen table, paying the bills.

Sue was turning every conversation toward the subject of James's teaching career lately.

"I guess… I don't really want to talk about it right now."

It was James's standard reply, and he could tell it was beginning to wear thin.

He knew that he and Sue needed to have a serious talk about the future, but putting it off for another day always seemed like a good idea.

The monotony of James's third year at Earl Warren was broken one beautiful spring afternoon in his last-period class of sophomores, which, although overcrowded, was a really good group of kids.

Most of the class was friendly and pretty mellow—and it was one of his more sociable, easygoing students that gave James some horrifying insight into just how dangerous everyday life was in the world in which his kids lived.

Deshawn Brown—who was certainly not the kind of kid that would ever look for trouble—shared with James and the class one spring afternoon the story of how he had accidently been shot during a drive-by shooting on the block where he lived.

"I was surprised at how it felt to get shot. It burned real bad. I didn't think it would burn like that," Deshawn said, proudly showing off his bullet wound—a long scar on his forearm—to the class.

As with James's previous student Alphonse Martinez, whose friend had been accidentally shot to death during James's first year of teaching, James didn't quite know what to say.

It turned out James didn't have to say anything as Deshawn's experience began a ten-minute class discussion about his students' experiences with gun violence in their neighborhoods. Several other students in the class had either witnessed shootings or knew somebody who had been shot or killed because of gun violence.

Carmen Vargas, who like Deshawn Brown was not the type of person who would ever seek out trouble, told the class how she had witnessed someone murdered—gunned down in the drug wars where her neighborhood was the disputed territory.

"There was so much blood—you couldn't believe it. And you could see the guy's insides coming out too. I was really messed up after seeing that. They sent me to counseling for a week."

"They should have sent you for more than a week," another student chimed in, reflecting James's reeling thoughts perfectly.

James would, after that class, spend considerable time thinking about Deshawn and Carmen and what life was like for them on a day-to-day basis. The normality of violence—gun violence, the constant threat of being jumped, and the constant presence of street gangs—was something people living in James's world only heard about on the news, if it made the news.

James wondered how many shootings and stabbings in New York City weren't even reported—how many acts of serious violence were ignored, just as the inner city and its children were routinely ignored.

And it occurred to James that the issue of basic safety had to be dealt with before meaningful progress could be made in educating the kids who had to live in those dangerous neighborhoods. He thought back to his introductory psychology class and remembered Abraham Maslow's theory of the hierarchy of needs that proposed that people must satisfy their basic needs—the need for safety being one of the most basic—before they are motivated to worry about less basic needs like their education.

When kids are worried every day about their physical safety and basic economic security, it seemed to James unlikely that such kids would worry too much about something as comparatively mundane as their grades. And James was again reminded of how powerless he was in the face of all the societal problems his kids faced, to make a real difference in their lives.

And it was James's understanding of, and sensitivity to, the many issues of violence that affected his kids that made him not want to send Tyrell Freeman to the Dean's office for acting out in class the day of the game of tag.

Tyrell was, like the rest of his sophomore class, a good kid, naturally affable, and someone James usually got along with quite well. But Tyrell had been acting out lately, unable to concentrate on his work, instead boasting to anyone who would listen about his fighting prowess, and demonstrating his skills by dancing around the room shadow boxing his imaginary foe.

James knew Tyrell was terrified.

Tyrell had been threatened by some gang or another—told he was going to get jumped after school for some reason or another. But, as usual, the particulars were unclear and Tyrell wouldn't supply any, so there was little anyone could do to protect Tyrell. And until the day of the game of tag, James had been generally successful in calming Tyrell down enough that he didn't feel the need to remove him from class.

But understanding the reasons for Tyrell's ever more frequent make-believe boxing matches wasn't the only reason James was hesitant to have him removed from class. It was an understanding of what it meant to send a kid to the Dean's office that gave James pause—and had caused James to have disruptive students removed only in the most extreme cases.

James had assumed that sending a student to the Dean's office at Earl Warren meant sending them to detention—something like a mandatory study hall that was supervised by a teacher or administrator.

This was not the case.

Removing a student from class at Earl Warren meant sending them to a "safe room," which was apparently "safe" because it was windowless and devoid of any books or other teaching materials that might cause any-one "harm."

It was also devoid of a teacher, and the kids that were sent there weren't encouraged to read or do homework… or to do anything at all. They just sat there, staring into space with vacant looks in their eyes—the way people might sit and stare into space when waiting to be called for jury duty or when stuck in a long line at the DMV.

James hadn't ever been to the "safe room" during his first two years at Earl Warren, and when he finally stumbled upon it in his third year at the school, he was disturbed by what he saw. So when James had Tyrell removed from class the day of the game of tag, it was only because James felt he had no other option available.

Tyrell had been shadowboxing again—because he had been threat-ened again—but unlike in previous bouts, James wasn't able to throw in the towel for Tyrell after a round or two. Tyrell just continued his boxing exhi-bition no matter what James did, dancing around the room, demonstrating the occasional "Ali Shuffle." But his punches were becoming wilder and wilder—to the point that James and some of his students were becoming concerned that Tyrell might accidentally hit someone for real.

So James reluctantly called security and had Tyrell removed for the day.

The class maintained its sanity for the next fifteen minutes or so, but whether it was all the excitement from Tyrell's earlier pugilistic exhibition or the silliness that sometimes happens at the end of the day on a beautiful spring afternoon, the class just fell apart.

What began as the inability to stay on task quickly devolved into laughing and singing and dancing, all of which quickly spiraled out of James's control—not that he had the energy at the end of the day and near the end of the school year, especially on such a beautiful spring afternoon to try to stop the madness.

"Tag, you're it!" someone behind James shouted at the top of his lungs.

James whirled around to see Tyrell Freeman, widely grinning as he faked James out with a fairly impressive move as he ran past him to tag another student, and the game of tag began.

Tyrell Freeman, to his credit, had discovered what had not occurred to every other student who had been removed from class during James's three years at Earl Warren—that the school's "safe room" was a jail without a jailer.

It wasn't as if there was a lock on the door or anybody paying attention to the students sent there—so Tyrell had simply got up and left—preferring to play tag with his friends in James's last class of the day than to sit in the "safe room" staring into space.

And as a wildly laughing Tyrell evaded being tagged by grabbing James from behind and using him as a human barrier between himself and the current "it," James could only laugh to himself at the absurdity of it all.

Fortunately, nobody saw the incident.

The class later apologized to James, and the game of tag they played that day would be their last. Thankfully, Tyrell was never jumped after school and, over the next several weeks, settled down and retired from boxing for the rest of the term.

But the game of tag showed James just how burned out he was, which was one of the reasons he had turned down the offer to stay on at Earl Warren—the offer of a tenured position.

Tenure in the New York City public school system could be granted after just three years—which was too short a period of time for anyone to know if they were going to be successful at any job, let alone being a teacher.

But more to the point, the system, after just three years, had worn James out.

Had he accepted the offer, James would have become a tenured teacher—a person with a job for life with good health insurance and a pension—no matter how apathetic he became about his career or about his students.

And James could see that he was already becoming disinterested and that in another couple of years, he would be like Norman Griffin—wandering the halls of Earl Warren, teaching his classes no more than competently, just waiting for the day he could retire with a full pension.

"You didn't even consider talking with me about it before you turned them down?"

Sue stood in the middle of their small living room, staring silently at James through her frizzy blond hair with a confused expression that was a mixture of anger and sadness.

James made a half-hearted promise to "talk about it later" before leaving for his nightly workout at the YMCA.

James began his four-thousand-yard swim that evening more aggressively than usual as he thought about all the frustrations in his life—his job, money… his marriage. James knew he and Sue needed to talk, but they didn't really talk that much anymore.

James swam faster.

He had made the right decision for himself—James was sure of that. But as he swam, he couldn't help thinking about all the less qualified people who would get tenure—all the people who wouldn't be as good of a teacher as he was or who weren't motivated by the desire to do good in the world but by the promise of lifetime employment with a pension and good healthcare; people who would make friends with their superiors and play the game well enough for three years to get the prize of a job for life—the prize of tenure.

All of which would have been just fine with James if there weren't innocent kids involved.

James increased his stroke count even further, making an aggressive flip turn off the pool wall at the deep end, propelling himself underwater with several dolphin kicks before emerging as an angry torpedo halfway down the lane.

The century-old pool at the YMCA was regulation length at twenty-five yards but sported only four narrow lanes in an elegantly tiled space, reminiscent of an ancient Roman bath. And apart from the occasional high school swim meet, it wasn't ordinarily used by people who could really swim—catering to an older crowd who mostly avoided James, letting him "do his thing" in the fast lane.

James was at an almost full sprint now, feeling the lactic acid building up in his muscles and the sensation of oxygen deprivation familiar to swimmers who push their bodies to their physical limits. He wouldn't be able to keep this pace for very much longer, and the rest of his workout would suck as a result of going out so quickly, but he didn't care. He needed to focus—to push himself as far as he could so he could forget about all the problems in the world... and all the problems in his life... and the only thing on his mind would be his swimming and the water and the pain...

Something was suddenly in James's way, and he crashed into it.

James bolted to his feet, towering over the frightened, elderly man who had wandered into his lane. "What the fuck are you doing?"

"I… I'm sorry. You came at me so fast… I didn't see…"

"You didn't see me…? Swimming here?" James was hyperventilating so badly he could barely speak. "You see that… sign? It says 'fast lane!' Can't you read? What… Are you stupid or something?"

The old man quickly left, leaving James standing alone, fuming, in the shallow end of his lane. But James's yelling had succeeded in attracting the attention of the lifeguard.

"Sir! There's no need for rudeness. We aren't used to people swimming…"

"Don't tell me how to fucking swim! When you can beat me in a race, then you can tell me how to fucking swim!"

The lifeguard lifted his hands in surrender, rolled his eyes, and walked away.

James retreated into the water, angrily swimming another few hundred yards at racing speed, only to stagger out of the pool several minutes later, dizzy and gasping for breath as he hurriedly made his way to his locker.

Afterward, James got the idea to go to a movie to kill some time as his outburst had cut his swim workout short and he didn't want to go home to face Sue.

James sat in the back of the theater, eating his bucket of overpriced popcorn, not really paying attention to the film except to note that Hollywood standards for screenplays had gone decidedly downhill—perhaps along with general literacy—audiences not seeming to take much notice of gaping plot holes, bad dialogue, one-dimensional characters, or sappy happy endings.

After the movie, James walked home.

It was three miles, but James wanted to make sure Sue was asleep so they wouldn't get into an argument. He couldn't handle another fight that evening, and now that the adrenaline had worn off, he felt a little sick to his stomach about how he had treated the old man and the lifeguard at the pool.

Tomorrow he would need to track them both down and apologize profusely.

When James did get home, he found Sue asleep far over on her side of the bed, which allowed James to sneak in without disturbing her. It was a great relief for James to be able to go to sleep that night and put off for yet another day the earnest talk he and Sue needed to have about the future.

CHAPTER 28

THE CHEATING SCANDAL

As James's third year drew to a close, he was again grateful for the break the Regents exams offered the faculty from the usual chaos that graced the halls of Earl Warren. The school was quiet now, and as James walked down one of its empty hallways on his way to the library where the faculty would begin their yearly routine of grading the English Regents exams, he could actually hear himself think, and his thoughts were saying—rather loudly—that he had chosen the wrong path in life and that it was time to turn around and backtrack as fast as he could.

He thought of Norman Griffin whom he had observed earlier in the day wandering the empty halls of Earl Warren after school—completely burned out—just going through the motions of teaching and waiting for the full city pension he would receive if only he could put up with the stress and the monotony for another five years. It was all Norman could talk about these days.

"Just another five years. Just another five years."

James knew he would be in exactly the same position as Norman if he decided to stay in the public school system. He could always transfer to a better school, and the quality of his job and the quality of his life would likely improve somewhat. But did he really want to continue? Did he really want to keep working in such a dysfunctional system? And was teaching really what he wanted to do for the rest of his life? He had become fairly good at it—but not excellent—not one of those "teacher of the year" types who was born to work with kids.

Not Martin Monty King.

James wondered what Martin was doing with his life. He hoped Martin had somehow found a way to become a teacher—or at least to work with kids in some other meaningful way. He wished he could find Martin and trade places with him because if there was one person who had the potential to make a difference in a place like Earl Warren, it was Martin Monty King—the guy the system rejected on the basis of a meaningless standardized test.

And James thought about his personal life—of his marriage to Sue.

The differences between James and Sue had caught up with the two of them. Perhaps Phil had been right all along—that James was one of them—an attorney meant to use his academic talents to navigate the legal landscape of the country for corporate America in his office back at the firm, dressed in his three-thousand-dollar suit. Sue certainly didn't belong in that world—and perhaps James didn't really belong in Sue's more traditional version of the world either.

The teachers had gathered around one of the tables at the library—Kevin going through his yearly routine of strongly reminding everyone that the grading rubrics "only" required this and "only" required that and that everyone needed to carefully consider the essays before failing a student.

"But I can't actually tell anyone what to do."

This really meant rationalizing passing students who—if an objective standard were applied—couldn't write anywhere near a high school level and deserved to fail the Regents. But those students were going to get a break—not just because they were Earl Warren students and because the faculty would generally want to give their own students the benefit of the doubt—but because Kevin's policy—and apparently the system's policy—was to lower the bar for these kids as far down as it could possibly go so they could move as many students through the system as possible.

Perhaps it was James's bad mood that day as he contemplated his life and his future, but it seemed to him that Kevin's insistence on easier interpretations of the Regents grading standards went even further this year—and that he was annoyingly repeating himself at every opportunity. James resented it more than usual, as he did the conflict of interest involved in grading his own students on what was supposed to be a standardized exam.

The grading itself was always fun, however, and put James in a somewhat better frame of mind. It was their yearly party, with everyone bringing a contribution of food or beverage with coffee and donuts on the English department's nickel as usual. And there was plenty of time for eating and casual socializing when taking a break from evaluating Regents exams. James and Leslie had been paired to grade together—and the two took turns making each other laugh as they pointed out to one another the more amusing mistakes in their student's essays.

Still, the two agreed most of the time that, under Kevin's stretched interpretation of the grading standards, the vast majority of the essays were good enough to pass. In truth, the papers James and Leslie read that day were good enough to pass less than half the time. But there were some essays that, even under the most benevolent grading system, were failing papers.

Keisha Sanders's incomprehensible submission was a good example.

Keisha had somehow stuck around long enough at Earl Warren to take a Regents exam. James was surprised she had—fully expecting her to become part of the unenviable statistic of high school dropouts the system produced in ever growing numbers at schools like Earl Warren. There had certainly been better students who had dropped out—a few of them, like Catalina Perez and Maria Rodriguez, had been, tragically, quite smart and talented.

Keisha, in contrast, didn't like or respect school. She wasn't curious or particularly bright, and James guessed she just stuck around for the social aspects of the place—not really caring whether she passed her courses or not—just hanging around because it was kind of fun to be in high school—and, perhaps, continuing to show up every now and then through simple force of habit.

It was clear from her Regents essay that Keisha simply wasn't educated; the fault for which could fairly be borne by many, including Keisha herself. She hadn't gotten an education from Earl Warren or any of the other schools she'd attended, and she hadn't bypassed the system and educated herself in any way. She couldn't write, she didn't understand the question or the reading attached to it, and most disturbingly, her paper confirmed what James already knew about Keisha after enduring her disruptive presence in two of his classes: after all the years she'd spent in the New York City public school system, she just couldn't think critically.

The procedure for a failing paper was that both Leslie and James had to agree—and that a third teacher would be needed to confirm the failure. Catherine was free to grade, and after a brief review of Keisha's work and an under-her-breath utterance of "Oh, dear Lord," the paper was put atop the small pile of failed exams.

And so went the process as it normally had. That was until the final day of grading was over and the cheating scandal—or non-scandal depending upon how you looked at it—began.

It was actually Catherine who first noticed and became so visibly angry that Leslie felt the need to restrain her slightly, although there was probably never any real danger of Catherine physically attacking Kevin.

Kevin, for his part, stubbornly stood his ground and continued his stare down of Catherine Angel until she finally relented, telling him in a soft, shaky voice that betrayed her outrage, "How dare you," before briskly exiting the library.

It was then that James noticed the failing paper pile was gone.

The grades had all been changed. Kevin had overruled them all. Every student who took an English Regents exam that year at underperforming Earl Warren High School had miraculously passed. And Keisha Sanders's paper was on the top of the new pile... with a new passing grade attached.

James was too stunned and tired to feel anything emotionally, but his analytical mind, trained to automatically question anything it couldn't easily wrap itself around, caused James to utter the single word of protest.

"But...?"

Leslie was quick to silently cut him off with an urgent shake of her head "No."

Although the question hadn't been directed at Kevin, he immediately turned his attention to James, saying tersely in a tone that was both firm and absolute, "It's final," before turning away and walking out of the room.

James never found out why Kevin regraded the papers—whether it was his idea or Principal White's or someone else's higher up. It didn't really matter. Legally it was a non-scandal. Written work was subjective, and the rubrics used to grade the work were also subject to interpretation. And the procedures used to grade the papers didn't seem to be written down anywhere, so Kevin was probably within his rights to overrule the process he himself had established. At least these were some of the arguments that ran through James's head as he analyzed the situation from a legal perspective.

This wasn't like some of the many cheating scandals that had been discovered and had rocked schools and school districts around the country. This wasn't a case where standardized test scores had been manipulated by teachers changing answers on bubble sheets or assisting students during exams or reviewing the exam questions with students before the exam—all in an effort to boost test scores—more often in underperforming schools and all for the professional gain of those in charge.

No—this was a more subtle kind of manipulation.

In a system where standardized test scores were such an important part of how both teachers and administrators were evaluated, it was no wonder there would be great incentive to influence those numbers in ways that could be gotten away with. And James wondered how common such practices were—and how common it was for such practices to remain undiscovered.

But the real scandal wasn't the changing of the scores on a few exams. The real scandal was that the majority of those students were going to graduate at all. The real scandal was that the system wasn't really about education—it was really about statistics. And James was reminded of the saying that there were three kinds of lies: lies, damned lies, and statistics—or in this case, grades, graduation rates, and standardized test scores.

Yes, high test scores, high grades, and high graduation rates are wonderful. Teachers love them, administrators love them, politicians love them, parents love them, and students love them. They tell a wonderful story of success and achievement—until you look behind the numbers and find out that few of those "high achieving" graduates can write, few can read with meaningful comprehension, and few know basic science or history or mathematics.

But if Earl Warren—or any school in such a system—were to graduate only half their senior class—or less—they would be out of business and people would lose their jobs. And there would be considerable anger and consternation from parents, and students, and politicians—all because such a school would actually be doing its job. All because such a school would actually be telling the truth.

And as James watched Keisha Sanders squeal with delight and jump up and down with her friends as she celebrated her passing score on the Regents exam posted on the English department bulletin board, James couldn't help but feel a little sick to his stomach.

Keisha turned her attention to James, who silently watched a short distance away as student after student checked the grade posting and got the happy news.

"I told you I would pass. You didn't believe me, mister," Keisha taunted James in her usual mocking tone.

"Yeah, Keisha, I guess you told me," James replied, just a little too dryly to get away with.

"Oh! Look," Keisha exclaimed, motioning to a few of her friends who were also celebrating their unlikely passage of the Regents exam. "He mad at me! Mister Hartman—he want me to fail! But I pass my Regents! I pass my Regents!"

Keisha sang the words over and over again derisively in James's direction.

James just walked away.

"Mr. Hartman!" Keisha called after him.

"You just got schooled, yo!"

James didn't look back.

There was some more laughter and a few more taunts thrown his way, but Keisha and her friends were too happy about their newfound academic success to pursue the matter further. And as James continued to walk away, he thought about how everyone, including himself, was really part of the great cheating scandal that went well beyond the Regents exam.

Every Regents prep class he had taught was part of that scandal—designed not to educate but to manipulate numbers on a standardized test to make the school look good. Every time James and other teachers passed students along in the system under pressure from administrators and parents and students—that was a cheat too. The dumbing down of standards, of assignments, of materials… It was all one great big cheating scandal—one great big lie. And the fact that all those students would graduate with a Regents degree for basically just showing up—that was the biggest cheating scandal of all.

And James understood, as he continued to walk away, that the system would be almost impossible to change because, despite all the noise people made about change whenever there was a revelation in the news that American students lagged far behind in global rankings of core subjects—or that the majority couldn't find England on a map and didn't know elementary facts about science or history or even about their own country—everyone really benefited from the great cheating scandal, and so long as the cheating wasn't too obvious, everyone, deep down, really didn't want to change a thing.

Students got their degree, and parents got a day to celebrate and be proud of their kids. Teachers and administrators got to keep their jobs. Politicians got to brag about the good numbers the schools were producing under their administrations.

The system made everybody happy—happy until the academic skills never learned were needed to pass a remedial English or math course at a community college or to meet the criteria for more than a minimum-wage job.

Leslie had told him as much with her constant mantra that teaching was about individual successes—that if a teacher could positively change the lives of just a few students in their entire career, their career had been a success.

And for Leslie—that was enough.

But for James, it wasn't enough, and so he walked away—away from Earl Warren and away from the teaching profession—and back along the road less traveled, which led James back to his mentor and friend Phil Blake, who, to James's great relief, was very happy to have him back at the firm.

EPILOGUE

James had originally planned on giving the apartment to Sue after the divorce and finding a small studio near the firm, but Sue hadn't wanted the property or any of the money James had tried to give her, instead insisting on moving in with a friend who lived in the Village.

And James was alone.

But he knew that Phil had been right about everything.

He knew Phil had been right even before he walked through the firm's great glass doors for the first time in three years. He knew Phil had been right even before he was greeted by the always happy and enthusiastic young receptionist at the front desk—always an aspiring actress or model or singer whose countenance and name would subtly change every year or two but who would be there forever to greet James and his colleagues with her attractive and reassuring smile at the start of each and every day.

He knew Phil had been right as he passed by his fellow associates as they worked at their desks in their shared offices, many of whom had barely noticed he had been gone. Nothing had changed. Every one of them looked, acted, and dressed the same as they ever had and the same as they ever would—the same as each other—which was the same as James. And being among them again made James feel happy and safe and at home for the first time in over three years.

Yes, the firm was a glorious palace of dark wood furniture and glass-walled conference rooms and freshly brewed coffee and delivered gourmet meals that were always billed to your clients. It was a fairy-tale kingdom that James would inhabit with people like himself and where life was predictable and comfortable and where everything was taken care of and where plenty of money could be made.

There was no dull cracking paint and old broken tile to look at, no eternal stench of urine around the bathrooms or big flying cockroaches or rodents living in your desk. No UFT or DOE or school administration imposing arbitrary rules and regulations. No horror stories.

James wondered why he had ever left. He was home.

James threw himself into his work. And again, Phil was right—James did have great potential as a lawyer. And without the notion that he should somehow be doing more good in the world and without Sue Ellen Bauer on his mind, he embraced his job completely.

Of course, Phil Blake was wrong about one thing.

It turned out Phil had only poor counsel to give when it came to women and relationships. Phil's wife of nineteen years finally divorced him in a rather messy and hard-fought affair, which eventually cost Phil a tidy sum of money, his house in the Hamptons, and his beloved Ferrari that he seldom had a chance to drive.

James met a similar fate a number of years later when his second wife, Jackie, a woman Phil had introduced him to with the highest of recommendations and who was a good friend of Phil's then wife, decided she'd had enough lonely nights and that it was time to cash in. And she did.

But it didn't really matter because James's life was the firm, and the firm was James's life. And James liked it that way. And he was very successful, at least within the confines of that small and narrow bubble.

As it turned out, James's experience as a teacher became one of his greatest assets.

He had, after all, spent three years of his life speaking publically in front of the most demanding of audiences. And although James wouldn't have admitted it to anyone, he understood privately that he had learned a lot from his students—in particular the subtle art of manipulation, which served him well throughout his career in both negotiations and the courtroom.

Apart from that, James wanted nothing more than to forget about his former students and their problems—and he especially wanted to put the dysfunctional world of public education out of his mind completely.

To that end, James made sure he saw less and less of Leslie. They would occasionally meet for coffee or lunch, but they really didn't have very much in common anymore, and James only pretended to listen to her stories of problem students or her complaints about the latest dictates coming from the DOE or Principal White.

James eventually got the excuse he needed to end their friendship completely in the summer of 2012 when the DOE finally decided, after so many years without academic improvement and with persistent school violence, including a well-publicized gang brawl in 2006 where two students were stabbed, that Earl Warren was, indeed, a failing school... and opted to shut it down.

Closing a school, according to the DOE, meant that everyone—both faculty and administration—would be reassigned so the school could reopen as a campus for several smaller high schools with entirely new staffs. Leslie was eventually reassigned to a high school in Brooklyn, and as she lived in Brooklyn, she had little reason to be in Manhattan on a regular basis. And James had little reason to venture out to Brooklyn.

The two met one last time after her reassignment for a quick coffee in October of 2012. Things were similar at her new school, Leslie complained, but with different people and a bit less of the chaos.

"There might be an opening next year if you're interested, Jim. The original five-year mission ended after only three—but there was a *next generation*, you know."

James politely declined. He was glad that Leslie seemed happy enough, and the two promised each other they would get together soon. They never did. And they never saw each other again.

Only one other incident briefly forced James out of his professional utopia and back into the world of public education. It was a chance meeting which affected him greatly but which he never shared with anyone.

It happened when James was on the subway—on the number two train heading downtown to 100 Center Street for a hearing in Supreme Court on a cold December Thursday about two months after James would see his friend and mentor Leslie Brooks for the last time.

Like the majority of New Yorkers, James had a love-hate relationship with the subway system. It was cheap, convenient, and easily the fastest way to get around, but unlike most other cities with subways, New York's was practically unavoidable, making it one of the most egalitarian places in the world, shared by the rich and famous as well as by the poor and the homeless.

It was James's luck that day that he had just barely made his train—squeezing himself and his briefcase through the closing doors at the very last second—but it was also James's misfortune that he happened to choose a car where a homeless man had made a row of seats his bed—where he had decided to "sleep in" for the morning rush hour.

James instinctively looked to move to the other side of the car to avoid the smell, but the car was already mostly full with the passengers already squeezed as tightly in the direction away from the homeless man as they could possibly go.

James was trapped until the next stop where he could switch cars.

James tried to look away from the decaying shell of a human being dressed in torn, soiled clothing—and he tried not to breathe as was his usual practice in such situations. But for some reason he was unable to turn away this time. There was something about this disheveled man—now slowly turning to face James while simultaneously scratching his privates through his barely attached pants—that held James's attention.

With his face now visible, James could see that the man had suffered a severe and disfiguring knife wound—the scar traveling down the center of his forehead, over his left eye and continuing down the left cheek for its entire length. It was a wide and hideous scar—a scar from a cut never attended to by a doctor and left to heal on its own under the most unsanitary conditions.

But the scar wasn't what had captured James's attention. What had captured James's attention was the man's age. Now that James could see his face, he realized the man was drastically younger than he had originally thought.

And when their eyes met, there was, to James's horror, recognition.

He could not conceal his shock nor could he look away from the shell of a man he knew to be his former student, Jimmy Wiggins. And James was now aware of a rapidly growing feeling of nausea creeping over him—and was also keenly aware that his legs were dangerously close to giving way beneath him as well.

Jimmy was staring at James now—his brow in the familiar furrow James recognized as the sign that he had gotten Jimmy's attention in class—but he didn't want his attention now. He wanted to be anonymous—to be gone.

Please don't remember me, James thought.

But it was too late. Jimmy Wiggins's growing smile revealed a maw of stained and missing teeth. And he uttered a single word. "Birthday."

The train slowed as it approached the next stop. And James had a decision to make. He had come to another major fork in the road of his life, and he had only seconds to make up his mind about which path to take.

There was a part of James who wanted to help Jimmy—a much larger part of James than he wanted to acknowledge. This wasn't some anonymous vagrant. This was someone James knew—still a kid, really—someone James had tried but failed to help. This was someone James had given his first... and probably his last... birthday party.

But if James were to stop and help Jimmy Wiggins... He cared—and that had made James Hartman a decent teacher—but James didn't want to care anymore. Caring meant dealing with Jimmy—a lost, decaying person whose stink made James gag and whose plight was probably without a solution anyway. And caring about Jimmy enough to try to help him could take days or weeks... or a lifetime.

And if James were to choose to care, where would it end? There were so many people like Jimmy Wiggins in the city—in the country—in the world. And the system—the school system, the economic system, the social safety-net system, bad parents, and our society generally—would produce more and more Jimmy Wigginses for people who cared to try to help.

It was impossible.

If James and his cohort of teaching fellows and an army of teachers and administrators—people who mostly cared—couldn't save one lousy public high school, then what was the point of trying? What was the point of caring at all?

The train stopped and James made his decision.

James staggered out of the car... and down the road *more* traveled by. He had to take a few minutes to recover, drawing the attention of several of his fellow commuters, one of whom offered to call James an ambulance, which James politely declined.

It was shortly after his encounter with Jimmy Wiggins that James started drinking.

It was never so much that it ever became a problem, but James made sure he drank enough so that he could forget more easily. He didn't want to care anymore—and whenever he started thinking about all the problems in the world—whenever he found himself "caring"—as was a part of his nature whether he liked it or not—his friend the dry vodka martini (or two or three) would be there to help him forget about such things and reset his mind back to focusing on the straight and narrow.

It was about a year after the incident with Jimmy Wiggins that by chance James met Sue Ellen Bauer—now Sue Ellen Henderson—pushing a stroller with her two-year-old daughter on Central Park West.

The two had barely spoken after the divorce, and if James had been thinking about life more than he permitted himself to, he might have marveled at how two people who had spent so many years together and had planned on having a family and growing old together could so quickly and so easily retreat back into their own separate worlds and become complete strangers to one another.

James had heard that Sue had, ironically, married a teacher and that the two had been expecting a child. But that was a couple of years ago, and now Sue and her smiling daughter were there in the flesh in front of James.

James had recognized Sue immediately.

She looked the same... only better—more radiant and happy as she laughed along with her daughter as she slowly pushed her along in her stroller. Sue didn't immediately respond to James's friendly wave—not because she held any animosity toward James but because it took her a moment to recognize her former husband.

Gone were the boyish good looks, the athletic build, and some of James's hair that was noticeably receding and beginning to gray in places. Not caring about the world had also meant not caring very much about himself—and James, for anyone who hadn't seen him in several years, was virtually unrecognizable.

Holding on to his youth was one of the many things James had chosen not to care about anymore. Indeed, the more he drifted away from his formative years, the more comfortable he became with his deteriorating appearance and ever-expanding waistline.

It was a relief, actually, not to be a young man anymore, and James embraced his newfound maturity and status. Why worry about unimportant things such as one's looks or whether one could still swim a competitive hundred-yard freestyle? What was the point? It was much less painful not to work out anymore and to eat whatever one pleased. And why worry about the problems of the world? James's youthful idealism—his empathy—hadn't solved anything. It had just caused him pain and three wasted years of his life.

So James forever gave up his beloved swimming soon after his return to the firm because swimming was something he had consigned to his youth—not that he had the time with all his professional responsibilities anyway. At first he had made a vague promise to replace it with morning push-ups and the occasional late-night workout on the treadmill in his building's gym—but those sentiments quickly went by the wayside.

The lack of physical activity had caused the pounds to quickly accumulate on James's person. He now sported a double chin and had a noticeable belly beneath his three-thousand-dollar suit, both of which would continue to grow for the remainder of James's life—fed by James's habit of eating a chocolate croissant or two with his morning latte and a fondness for late-night moo shu pork delivery from the Empire Szechuan if he was working especially late at the firm—which was often.

Adding to his unhealthy appearance was James's complexion, which had become unnaturally pasty from spending so little time outdoors and which made his dark facial hair stand out in a five-o'clock shadow even when freshly shaven.

James and Sue exchanged pleasantries. It was clear they really had nothing in common anymore. Sue and her new husband had plans to move out of the city so they could raise their daughter, Mary Grace, in the country where she always seemed so happy—and where they could afford to buy a real home where they could have more children and live a comfortable life together.

James wished her well.

And James said goodbye to little Mary Grace who, if James had made different choices in his life, might have been his own daughter. But Mary Grace wasn't paying any attention to James. She was very busy with her newest toy—a mermaid princess who lived in a little bottle of enchanted seawater from her magic kingdom under the sea.

And as Mary Grace lifted the princess out of her bottle and held her up to the afternoon sky, she carefully blew air into the thin film of shimmering magical liquid that delicately clung to the mermaid princess's tail.

Mary Grace's eyes opened wide—and she grinned—and then laughed with pure happiness as she watched the miraculous bubbles she had made glisten in the sun as they floated on the air toward the strange man in the blue suit who was trying his best to fake a smile.

"Bubbles!" she exclaimed.

James said his final goodbyes. He stood for a moment on that beautiful fall day in New York City on Central Park West to watch Sue and little Mary Grace disappear around the corner of a luxury apartment building.

Bubbles… James thought as he straightened his tie. *How childish.*

And he headed back to the firm.